T. B. PHILLIPS
Creepy Creations

Based on the hit comic series *Ferryman Tales* by
Chris Hays & McLain McGuire

ANDALON
PRESS

Ferryman
Creepy Creations, Book One

Published by Andalon Press
Copyright © 2022 by T.B. Phillips

Cover design by Lynnette Bonner of Indie Cover Design, images ©
  Cover illustration used by permission of Charter Comics
  Illustration #1 Shipwreck by D.J. Hall used by permission of Charter Comics
  Illustration #2 Ferryman by D.J. Hall used by permission of Charter Comics
  Illustration #3 by Muamal Khairi used by permission of Charter Comics
  Illustration #4 by Muamal Khairi used by permission of Charter Comics
  Illustration #5 by Joseph Scott used by permission of Charter Comics
  Illustration Coloring by Matt Chambers
  Torch graphic by Vecteezy.com
Book interior design by Stewart Design, https://StewartDesign.studio

ISBN 978-1-7331805-9-7

This is a work of fiction. Names, characters, places, and incidents are a product of the author's imagination. Locales and public names are sometimes used for atmospheric purposes. Any resemblance to actual people, living or dead, or to businesses, companies, events, institutions, or locales is completely coincidental.

Emma,
Don't Pai
the
Ferryman!

Take the Coins
Two at a Time,
Not One, nor Three,
No More, No Less.

For Passage of Fate,
The Fare is Exact.
For a Ferryman's Price,
The Wrong Fare is Death.

PART I
EXACT PAYMENT

PROLOGUE

Castle Hills Point, 1580

A tempest raged with violence, frothing the sea amidst angry waves. Upon those a ship swayed first port then starboard, tossing fore and aft. Its timbers barely held. The crew held on as well, seasoned and used to storms, but never one so close to rocks. The strongest-willed remained on deck, peering into the night and watching for anything upon which they could run aground.

"Hazard, three points starboard!" the lookout called.

The helmsman reacted, turning the wheel hard to port and compensating six points on the compass. His palms sweated—a miscalculation would kill them all. A gust of wind came; one he hadn't anticipated. It pushed the sails too far to port, tipping the masts and causing the ship to list even farther. Luckily, the master sailor reacted with calmness and righted the vessel without taking on water.

"Steady on!" the captain ordered. "We'll be free of this inlet and on to Newfoundland by morning!" But the storm had another destination in mind for the *Drake,* forcing it toward shallower waters. Jean Le Sage faltered, suddenly unsure of his route. The seas were too high to judge their breaks and, if miscalculated, the ship would lose its main mast.

Lightning flashed overhead, striking the crow's nest and sending lookouts flying from their perch. Another strike hit the bowsprit, cracking the heavy timber in half and lighting it aflame.

During a third flash, Le Sage peered northward, spying a natural harbor offering protection from the heavier swells and crippling winds. He made up his mind and pointed the way for the helmsman. The man nodded, turning into a large wave and allowing it to push them along their way.

We're saved, thought the captain, reaching into his pocket and drawing out two coins. Staring toward the inlet he held them up to his eyes, looking through the golden discs and out through the staring eyes of the skulls minted on the face. He abruptly pulled them away, terrified by the vision he had seen. He turned, screaming a new heading to his helmsman.

The sailor, now gripping the heavy wheel and bracing his legs against its desire to spin freely, stared back at his captain with a look of horror. Another flash from above revealed what the captain had seen. Instead of safe haven, only crippling rocks awaited *Drake* and her crew.

"Come about!" Le Sage commanded. His voice lost its strength to the storm. "Full to starboard!"

But the wheel would not turn the way he hoped, and the helmsman's efforts to hold it steady proved in vain. The heavy oak ripped free from his grip and spun hard to port, one of its handles striking the back of his head with force.

Jean Le Sage briefly watched his helmsman bleed out on the deck then unlashed himself from the rail and made his way to gain control of the massive wheel. Another wave tossed *Drake*, splashing a heavy wave across her deck, cleansing it of both blood and captain. Without human hands to guide her, the galleon rushed into the bay, crashing its hull along a rocky shoal.

Castle Point, Rhode Island Colony, 1637

The storm had mercilessly pounded the peninsula most of the night, shaking the farmhouse and threatening to flood its interior. The family within had barely slept, only offered respite just before dawn. But the rooster crowed and the farmer awakened, ready to start his day despite his lack of rest. Determined, he made his way to Castle Point, named so for the rugged wall of rocks protecting the rich farmland just east.

As expected, the storm had stirred up the ocean floor, revealing new riches and thrust them onto the beach. An ancient shipwreck had been among this bounty, a hulking heap of lumber laying atop the shoal. Seamus Flannigan hurried down the slope, careful not to lose footing atop the slippery rocks. Heedless of the icy waters, he waded out to inspect this offering from God, a gift from providence, just like the name of the founding city of the colony.

As Seamus approached the wreckage, he found what had once been part of the forecastle, a charred hunk of timber floating past. He frowned at the name, reading it several times in his head. *Drake*.

God had delivered the legendary wreckage of Jean Le Sage to Rhode Island.

He hurried home to Molly eager to share a tale of riches waiting to pluck from the sea.

Together, they ventured down to claim the bounty provided by their lord. They prayed over the riches, a harvest unlike any other they had found. Then they prayed for a different reason, asking for their God to free them from a burden resting alone in an ancient chest. Unlike the others, this was made of lead, heavy and weighing down a portion of the ship itself against the rocks. Husband and wife knelt over it, lifting the lid and peering inside, only to gasp at the evil it contained.

Their prayers that night were a petition, pleading for protection against what would surely prove a plague against their family.

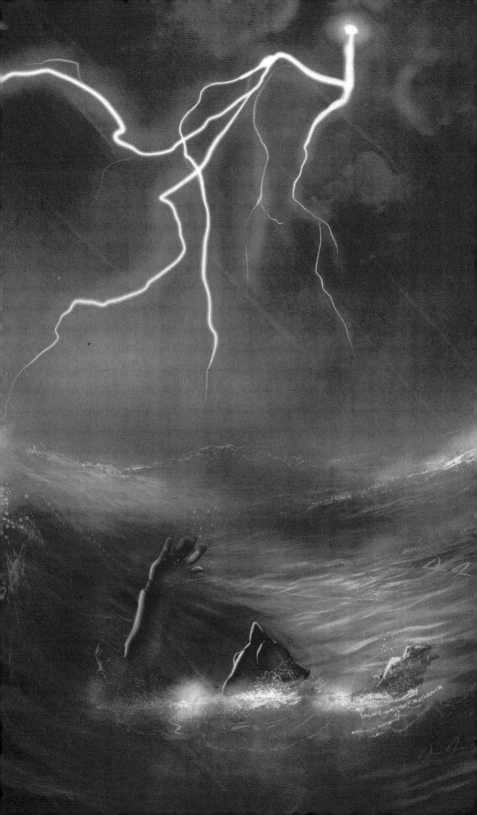

CHAPTER ONE

Castle Hills, Rhode Island Colony 1694

Curtis Charles stared at the bottom of his mug. He had come for one and no more, but his friend William Mayes had convinced him to stay for several. It felt good, the devil's brew taking over his mind and replacing apprehension with courage. He rapped knuckles for another and the tavern maid poured.

"Tell us a story, Ann," William begged, holding up a coin.

"What kind of story have I to give *you*?" the woman laughed. "I know what tale you want, but won't speak of patrons, no matter *what* you pay! Your father would toss me out onto the streets."

Curtis stared up at the woman, beautiful and buxom with blonde locks that curved around her cheeks and rested on a bosom too large for her frame. "Don't tell us about any of *them*, then," he pleaded, hoping to find another way to ask about the famous pirate. "Tell us of riches and treasure!"

Ann looked left then right, leaning in with a smile. "You want riches and treasure?" she asked with a wink.

"Tell us," William begged. "Aren't you friends with him? Don't you know the captain? I heard father slip that he came in here."

"Know him?" Ann roared with laughter. "I be *knowin'* him for sure, if beddin' him you mean!" The waitress pulled up a chair, leaning both elbows on the table and sitting like a man with knees spread wide.

Curtis blushed, a glance tempting him to stare wantonly at the pale skin peeking out above her knee. He refused, forcing his eyes deeper into the mug while his thoughts turned to Mary Griggs. Though her mother was keen on him, the girl had not yet agreed to marriage and would not until he proved his ability to provide for a family. It was time to nail down a real career and focus.

"Is it true he's setting out for another voyage?" William pressed. "I've heard he's earned another marque, this time for privateering in the Arabian Sea!"

"You looking to join his crew, William?" Curtis asked, shocked by his friend's boldness. The older boy had run away several years earlier and joined up with William Kidd's crew. But only his father, the owner of the tavern, and Curtis Charles knew that, and Ann Mason of course.

"No! Not at all!" Mayes lied. The young man yearned for more adventure.

"William Mayes Junior," Ann jeered, "I don't detect a bit of coward, do I? Did you see too much of the big, bad world?"

"Of course not!" William stood, but the ale betrayed him, losing balance as he dropped back into the chair. "I'm a fisherman, not a pirate!"

"What about *you*, Curtis Charles?" Ann demanded.

"I don't venture off dry land," he replied solemnly, throwing back the contents of his mug in a single swig.

"Oh," she teased, "so *you're* the coward!"

"Don't call him that!" William cut in, coming to his friend's aid. "Don't you know what happened to his pa?"

"I don't know, and I don't care," Ann proclaimed.

"He ran the Bristol Ferry," Curtis said quietly, handing the mug over to be refilled. "He died when I was a boy. A storm brewed while we rounded Prudence Island. We were trapped, unable to press forward or turn back after the waves rolled."

Ann had lost all sense of humor at the tale and filled his mug and slid it over without a word, silently waiting for more.

"He died, my pa, saving me. I won't go out on it at all now. So yeah, I guess I'm a coward."

"I.. I don't blame you," Ann said with more than a hint of empathy. "I wouldn't either." She pointed at his mug. "This round's on me."

"We should go," William suggested.

"No," Ann begged. "I'm sorry I treated you so. Please stay, I'll tell you that story I promised."

"Of Captain Tew?" William asked with excitement.

"No, I said I won't speak of him. As promised, I'll tell you a story of treasure. There's been much of it here in Rhode Island. Let me tell you about the *Drake*."

"I've not heard of the *Drake*," Curtis replied thoughtfully. Rhode Island had always been a haven for pirates, long before Thomas Tew claimed the harbor as his sanctuary.

"She were a four-masted beast, long and wide with twelve pounders ready to crack the timbers of her prey. She were captained by the fearsome Jean Le Sage."

"A Frenchmen? In Rhode Island? What would a papist be doing in a Quaker colony?"

"Ah!" Ann grinned wildly. "But this was before the colony, during the Huguenot uprising! He'd been preying upon the Spanish to the south and *Drake* swam fat with Incan gold! His lust for coin unquenched, Le Sage found one of her majesty's ships off St. Kitts and took her as well! But, unbeknownst to him, the box he'd stolen belonged to none other than Queen Elizabeth's own astrologer, the occultist John Dee!"

Curtis felt his blood run cold at mention of the name. Stories of John Dee had been revived in recent years, especially with the recent trials in Salem. Many a woman had been burned or dunked in the colonies, and church leaders pointed at Dee's writings as a source of the problem.

"The gold was cursed," Ann went on, "minted for Dee's followers and full of voodoo magic from the islands. But Le Sage was of the dark arts, himself! He knew what he had and worked his own ritual to remove the curse. Believing he could keep it for his own, he fled north toward Newfoundland."

"What happened then?" William asked.

"A great storm grew upon the Atlantic, a raging tempest of evil origins, confused by the power struggle of two magics. Dee's curse held onto the gold, but Le Sage's twisted and fought against it, whipping the sea around his vessel into a frenzy! They crashed against Castle Hill, the very spot the lighthouse stands today!"

"And the gold?" Curtis asked, dreaming of the riches and how he could finally ask for Mary's hand in confidence.

"Lost forever," Ann said with a shrug, "but there *are* rumors." She leaned in, eager to spread her conspiracy. "It's known among us women that there's a coven of witches near Castle Hill."

Curtis sat up straighter, the ale no longer gripping his mind as tightly as before. *The Griggs' farm is near there!*

William must have had the same thought and suggested, "Maybe we *should* call upon your sweet Mary tonight? She may've seen witches in her fields!" He erupted with laughter, but Ann's eyes locked with Curtis's. There was no humor in either pair.

"Are you suggesting," Curtis asked her flatly, "my Mary may be a witch?"

"Stranger things have proved true," the barmaid said with a shrug. "Margaret Murphy was accused and burned for her sins. Perhaps your Mary's guilty as well."

"I've heard enough," Curtis decided, standing to leave. He staggered slightly from the ale, but his mind remained clear. He would leave before hearing lies about his love.

"Rose Sadler," Ann said flatly, causing both young men to pause. "I heard it from Rose Sadler that both Mary and her mother, Elizabeth, are witches."

"Rose Sadler was executed for witchcraft six months ago," Curtis said over his shoulder. "When did she tell you this?"

"Just before. She claimed to be of their coven, but they gave *her* up as a scapegoat so they could carry on. Rose told me that, if any accusations were made about her, to know it was the Griggs."

"I won't believe it," Curtis said.

"Did she leave proof?" William demanded.

"She knew the whereabouts of Le Sage's treasure. Claimed it was on the Griggs' farm, hidden in a cave beneath the lighthouse."

"Nonsense," Curtis exclaimed, making his way to the door. He'd had enough and stormed out into the night.

The heavy wood slammed behind him, just as the night air entered his lungs. The shock of it did little to clear his mind, now fully muddled by the ale. *Those lies,* he thought, *are too much to believe.*

He wandered aimlessly, uncaring about direction, his steps driven by a desire to move further away from the accusations. *Ramblings of a condemned woman,* he reasoned, *lies told to take down others and save herself.* But then he wondered, *Could Mary actually be a witch?*

Curtis abruptly found himself on the waterfront, a place he tried so hard to avoid, and froze in his tracks. Everything around the boy reminded him of grief he had put aside and how much he hated the water. Tall ships stood all around, their sails tied securely while the vessels rested. Below decks, their crews either slept in their hammocks or had moved ashore for a night of pleasure. The rows of masts proved overwhelming, forcing him to face that fateful night when he lost his pa. He fell to his knees and retched, reliving the moment as if it had only just occurred.

What had begun a quiet night three years earlier turned
fearsome. Curtis served as deckhand and helped with the rowing
when needed, with his father navigating Narragansett Bay and
working the sails like a master. Six souls rode the Bristol Ferryman
that night, usually an uneventful crossing. But, on this night, the
winds erupted fiercely, coming out of nowhere and nearly ripping
the small sail from the tiny craft. It was built for harbors and inlets,
not for storms or open water, and tossed about wildly while the
people onboard panicked.

"Rest easy!" Pa had shouted over the howling gale, consoling
his fare. They were a small family, with a husband, wife, and two
small children. "Tie off!" he commanded, but they were people
accustomed to life on land, and the order proved meaningless.

Curtis had helped them, seeing their confusion at the order.
Though only fifteen at the time, he was a master sailor like his
father. He knelt beside the children, tying perfect bowline knots
to keep them secure in case of the worst. Then he did the same for
the wife and finally the husband.

"I'll do it myself!" the man had growled, pushing the teen
away. He was full of anger as if the ferryman were at fault for the
storm. But he pushed too hard, sending the teen toppling backward.

Curtis could not fight against the sensation of falling,
endlessly flailing his arms as he tumbled untied over the side. His
entire stomach sank as he fell, gasping for air as he toppled over,
plunging into the icy bay. It stung then, biting at his skin and gripping his chest with vicelike cold. He gasped, but thankfully was
too out of breath to take another. Had he breathed in he would
have drowned immediately.

Fighting against the angry water, he choked and spat the salty
foe from his lips, sending it spraying upward. His boots, heavy
for cold sailing, dragged him under and young Curtis closed his

eyes tightly. Death loomed, he knew, and threatened to take him that very night.

But strong hands suddenly gripped him, heaving upward. He sputtered and gasped once more, this time drawing the sweetness that promised life. He felt his father's frantic effort, tying a line around his son's waist. Curtis gripped the hempen rope, clutching it with ten fingers now white with desperation, and heaved himself toward the ferry now tossing about. Only the family was aboard, and their terrified eyes watched the water behind the teen.

He scrambled aboard quickly, untying the bowline and ready to toss a lifesaver to Pa. As he turned, he realized his father was gone—taken by the sea and buried forever beneath its icy froth. He yearned to fall to his knees, to mourn the man who gave him life not only once but twice, but shouts of terror turned his attention. The small vessel, now adrift without hands on the rudder, raced toward a rocky shoal. With a mighty heave, he grabbed the rudder and pulled it toward starboard, trying desperately to steer portside. They narrowly survived.

Back in Newport, Curtis opened his eyes but gasped from the memory, reliving the icy fear. He had beached the craft, settling the family in and camping on Prudence Island for the night. The next day they had continued on to Bristol to finish the fare. Curtis Charles had returned to Newport without his pa, but never stepped foot on a boat after that, swearing off the sea and selling the vessel to another ferryman.

Fully recovered, the young man stood to his full height. With his feet firmly set upon dry land he was safe from this memory for another stretch of time and began his drunken journey westward of Newport.

"I have to know," he spoke into the night, turning his feet toward Castle Hill, "if Mary Griggs is a witch or not." As he left the docks Curtis Charles paused, grabbing an iron torch meant for those working on the pier. It wasn't stealing, these things were a dime a dozen to the dock workers, and he would need it if he found the cave Ann had mentioned.

Footsteps pounded as a young man approached, startling Curtis Charles who held the torch like a weapon.

"There you are!" William Mayes proclaimed out of breath, moving closer to the waving flame. "I wondered where you'd gone." Then he frowned. Recognizing determination written on his friend's face, he asked, "Where are we going?"

"To confront Mary," Curtis explained, "then to find a treasure."

CHAPTER TWO

Griggs' Farm stood atop the ridge, overlooking both town and harbor. Not far away, only about half a league, stood Castle Hill and the lighthouse named for the highest point in Newport. The light of it burned, marking hazards for ships entering or leaving the cove. It served as a beacon for Curtis and William as they climbed the road.

"Her mother's likely to run you off at this late hour," William warned. "We should go straight ahead to the cave!"

Curtis Charles gave him a look that meant warning, his friend sailed a rocky channel with those words. "Her mother approves of me," the young man insisted.

"Maybe so, but her father's likely to plow you under his field if you wake him."

"Her father wants his daughter married," Curtis replied. He could see the farmhouse now, the windows flickering with light lit within. "And it appears they're awake. That light's coming from the kitchen, so they won't be averse to visitors."

The pair trekked the final steps carefully, each very much aware of how much they'd drank, not wishing to draw unnecessary attention to their drunkenness. Good Christians of Rhode Island preached tolerance but never for drunks who banged on their doors in the dark of night. When they finally reached the door, Curtis held out a shaky hand and did just that.

Mary immediately answered the door. She seemed out of breath, as if she had rushed to answer. Seeing Curtis Charles and

William, she gasped. "What are you doing here?" Her voice was pleasant enough, but irritation found its way into her tone.

"I had to see you, Mary, I..." Curtis began.

The girl recoiled immediately with hand over nose and mouth. "You smell like a brewery, Curtis Charles!"

"I had a few, Mary, but I'm not bad off-drunk. I walked most of it off." He leaned against the frame, his torch moving dangerously close to the thatch roof.

"Step away with that thing!" Mary cried.

Curtis backed up immediately, ashamed of his clumsiness.

"Who's at the door, Mary?" a woman asked from within. Curtis recognized her as Elizabeth, the girl's mother. The pair were nearly identical, only a decade and a half apart.

"Curtis Charles and William Mayes, Mother. But they're just leaving." Mary insisted. She shot them both a look of warning, as if they should comply immediately.

The door opened wider and the older version of Mary stepped into the entryway. "If you've come calling on my daughter, you've done so at too late an hour, Curtis. You'll have to come back tomorrow."

"I'm sorry," he begged. "I heard some awful things in the tavern, rumors I thought you should hear from me."

The woman and girl exchanged a look, then Elizabeth smiled disarmingly. "Let me guess. Ann Mason has been spreading stories about us being witches? We've been down this path when Rose Sadler and Margaret Murphy were condemned. Both the constable and magistrate know we're devout Christians and already tossed out those accusations. We appreciate your concern, but we're fine. Please go home and we'll talk again tomorrow."

"I'm sorry, Mrs. Griggs," Curtis begged as the door shut between them.

"C'mon," William said, tugging his friend's suspenders and half dragging him away. Once they were out of sight of the house, he pulled him to the ground. "Douse the torch!"

"What?" Curtis demanded, suddenly angry at the act. "Why'd you do that?"

"We're *not* leaving, we're doubling back to follow them. They're up to something, I *know* it! It's almost midnight, yet they're fully dressed. And how did Farmer Griggs sleep through her screaming when you almost burned the house? I don't like it, Curtis. We need to follow them!"

Curtis reluctantly put out the torch, but instead of tossing it aside, he clutched it like a weapon close to his body. What William suggested was dangerous, especially if Mary and her mother turned out to be *actual* witches.

The young men crept closer, crawling on the ground and staying low beneath the fence line. They watched, waiting for the light in the kitchen to extinguish. After about twenty minutes, it did. The front door opened, and two hooded figures hurried outside and moved toward the lighthouse. William nodded and quickly followed, leaving Curtis to decide what to do. He wanted so badly to believe Mary was innocent, but seeing a pair of figures leaving the house allowed doubt to flood in.

He took off running after William.

The hooded figures slowed as they reached the lighthouse, then picked their way carefully down the cliffside. The young men paused before following, watching unseen while memorizing the path. As the figures disappeared behind some rocks, William stepped forward. He climbed several feet down before realizing Curtis hadn't followed. He looked up, finding his friend's eyes full of fear.

"Well? Are you coming?"

Curtis stared down at the waves crashing against rocks below and once more remembered the night his father died. He was too close to it, that ruthless and unforgiving sea.

"Don't be a coward!" William hissed.

"I don't know if I can *be* anything else," Curtis Charles muttered, then took a breath and carefully stepped out onto the ledge. From here it seemed a bit wider than it had from above, so he slowly made his way downward. The trail proved easier than he expected, well-tended as though often travelled. *By whom?* he wondered. *Witches?*

Up ahead, William waved with excitement. He had found the entrance to the cave. Curtis joined him as quickly as he dared, looking into the void and hearing voices echo back. The rhythmic chant was incomprehensible, like a foreign language spoken repeatedly. The young men made out two words.

"Eirigh suas!" women's voices proclaimed. "Eirigh suas! Eirigh suas!"

Then deep moaning came from a man, followed by a woman's scream. In all, the sounds told a story of pain before abruptly falling quiet.

"It sounds like a ritual," William whispered. "We should go for help!"

"I don't know," Curtis argued. "We've no proof of what they're doing down there." He thought of Mary and her mother, realizing they may not be guilty of witchcraft at all. They may simply be midnight cave explorers, bat watchers, or something else just as crazy. *No,* he thought, *they* had *to be witches.* He handed over his torch to William. "Go back," he finally said, "and I'll go in. If they catch me, they know I'm in love with Mary and might believe I'd keep my mouth shut for *her.*"

William nodded, almost relieved, and clutched the torch tightly to his chest. "Good luck," he offered. Then he quickly crept his way up the rocks above, leaving his friend behind.

Curtis swallowed. He'd already come too far to turn back, and so he pressed onward.

The cave was wetter than expected, and the walls dripped with moisture, so it was a miserable hike. He had to be careful not to lose his footing, but quickly fell into an effective gait that maintained balance. Thankfully the moonlight outside aided him most of the way until so deep it no longer helped. Then he slowed, the passage eventually turning downward, arching slowly to the left and plunging him into total darkness. He crept carefully the rest of the way, rounding a bend. He stepped out onto ledge, finding himself fully exposed and standing atop a grand descent into a larger cavern.

The bottom of it matched sea level, and a perfectly smooth pool lay still without wave nor ripple. In front of this stood five hooded figures deep in a ritual, looming over a strange symbol. Several torches lined the shoreline, illuminating the water with flickering light. It was deep, about twenty feet, and lined on all sides by smooth walls.

Curtis ducked down behind some rocks to his right, confident he was hidden, and watched the figures closely. At their feet was drawn a symbol, a five pointed star within a circle, carefully scratched in the sandy floor and filled with a crimson liquid. *Blood,* he realized, as his eyes focused on the goat lying in the middle of the symbol. Its lifeless eyes stared at the pool of water.

"Shíolraigh agus ardú," one of them said in a woman's voice, and the others chanted loudly in response.

"Eirigh suas!" they proclaimed.

The women repeated their chorus with arms raised above the pool for several minutes, and Curtis watched their hoods closely for any slight offering of recognition. One did finally slide back, and he was shocked to learn Elizabeth Griggs led the ritual.

"Shíolraigh agus ardú," she repeated, stooping over the carcass to remove something dark from within. With arm outstretched over the pool, she held the animal's heart, dripping hot blood over the tranquil water.

"Eirigh suas!" the others murmured quietly now, hushed with excitement by what was to come.

Curtis brimmed with excitement as well. Though frightened, he eagerly witnessed the dark ritual. He had no idea what to expect going further and marveled at the possibilities. He, like the goat, never took his eyes from the pool, watching as a dark shadow suddenly appeared in its depths. Whatever, or whoever, it was, swam from a hidden passage beneath the pool. The once glasslike surface splashed wildly with the emergence of a man.

Josiah Griggs swam toward the witches, tightly clutching something in his left hand while emerging from the shallows. He waded toward the waiting figures. One of them stepped forward and her hood slid back revealing Mary. The girl handed a robe to her father. He, in turn, handed over something small to his daughter. His vacant eyes seemed not to recognize her, nor to even seem aware of his surroundings. He blankly stared as if incapable of thought.

At her mother's prompting, Mary held up two coins, shining golden in the torchlight. She raised them to her eyes as if seeing through the gold. After another whisper from her mother, she chanted, "Atropos, Clotho, and Lachesis!" She paused, listening as her mother gave her the rest of the incantation, then recited, "I am your servant, a slave to the fates and blind to your secrets. Reveal them now. Show unto me the lessons from Manann." At first nothing seemed to happen, but then the girl gasped. "I see it, Mother! It's as you promised!"

"What do the fates show you, Daughter? Tell us, now, as you see!"

"I... I do not marry, not Curtis Charles nor *any* man! I'm a spinster! Someone else lives in a grand home at Castle Hills, but it isn't me. I'm... I'm in a different *kind* of home for those who've lost their wits!" Mary began to tremble, her fingers shaking as she held the coins to her eyes. "I see... fire! Flames as high as treetops! Oh, Mother, it's our home! Our house and barn burn as we speak! Our fortune is taken, stolen by he who started the fire!"

"Calm, child. Since you've seen these fates there's time to prepare and change them. When does the fire occur?"

Mary let out a whimper, dropping the coins. They bounced and rolled on the rocks, one of them disappearing into the void and sending tiny ripples to disrupt the once again still waters. The other landed near her mother's feet. The girl keened, sliding to her knees and letting out a wailing cry. "Now, Mother! The fire burns *now!*"

Elizabeth picked up the other coin from the rocks, gripped it angrily then tossed it into the water beside the other. "If this is our fate, then we must face it at once and turn its tide." She and the others took off running at once, forgetting Farmer Griggs standing by the pool. The woman stopped right next to Curtis as she reached the cavern entrance, calling for her husband. Without even blinking, he followed without urgency, a ghost of a man lost in his trance and seeing only whatever reality she seemed to have placed in his mind. Only then did Josiah follow, strolling past Curtis as he hid.

The boy let out a sigh of relief. Elizabeth had stood so close. He waited until the count of thirty, then stood, moving to the water's edge. Kneeling, he drew the two coins out of the water, disturbing the surface and sending a ripple across the cavern. He held them up, marked with strange letters around the edges. He stared at the image of a skull smiling back from the center. *Smiling?* he pondered. *Or laughing?* He slid them into his purse and tied it securely.

His legs no longer belonged to Curtis, and the invisible pull overwhelmed his fear of drowning. They carried him forward into the water, fueled by mysterious curiosity pulling him deeper. *There's a passage beneath this cavern, and it leads to wherever Josiah found these coins.* The lure of treasure proved too strong for reason, and he breathed deeply before disappearing beneath the surface.

CHAPTER THREE

Curtis kicked himself awake, tossing, turning, and throwing off sheets. He sat upright, heart thumping as if trying to escape his chest. The deafening pain between his ears reminded him of flagons of ale he should have avoided the night before, and he accepted misery with defeated surrender. This hangover was real and here to stay.

His state of undress reminded of a different problem, and he bolted upright with remembrance. *I swam beneath the cave!* It all felt dreamlike, but there, hanging above the warm hearth, were his drying clothes. They had been there awhile, and most of the fire had already burned down. One of his socks had fallen, singed after landing in the coals. It was his only pair, and one less meant none at all the next day, at least until he could buy a new pair.

Coin. He needed coin to buy new socks, and most of his was spent on drinks the night before. *Coins.* Another problem leapt into his memory, and Curtis scrambled to his feet.

The reason my clothes were soaked!

He had fully submerged himself, diving downward into the pool and feeling the rocks for an opening. He found it, a narrow gap one he would not have noticed had Josiah not emerged from that very spot. The underwater tunnel led him deeper underground.

His time below passages had been terrifying, swimming in total darkness for nearly a minute. He had begun to fear there was no cavern on the other side, but soon he caught a dim glimpse of light overhead. He emerged from the water gasping for air. After going without for so long, it tasted oddly sweet.

I nearly drowned! he realized, thinking once more of his father.

The second cavern was tiny, barely big enough for two men to stretch their arms out to their sides. It was tall, open at the top with a crack too narrow for a man to crawl through. Moonlight entered easily, though, flooding down upon a grand sight. Just ahead on the rocks sat a chalice, full of coins like those Mary and her mother had dropped into the water. Below that rested an open chest, full to the brim with the same wealth.

Curtis found his footing, heaving himself from the pool and scrambling toward the waiting treasure. Overhead, water sprayed down like icy mist, the result of the bay crashing against the shore. He had shivered, both from the temperature and excitement.

The swim back had proved treacherous, risky while carrying that chest—heavy and nearly impossible to haul. But determination has a way of pushing a man beyond his brink, and he somehow managed to heave it to the other side. He had almost left the cave, eager to haul his treasure home, but paused to cover his tracks. Curtis Charles dropped two coins in the water in case Mary went looking for hers. He wanted to leave no trace he had been there.

Now, in his apartment, Curtis scrambled to his closet to check on his haul. Timidly sliding the chest from its hiding place, he carefully opened the lid. Inside rested thousands of the golden coins. He shivered once more, but not from remembrance of the swim. This time he was certain the skull marked upon them laughed, amused by his foolish greed.

Curtis Charles had become a wealthy man overnight. All he had to do was hide this treasure from his friends, but especially from Mary. *Mary,* he thought. *The witch.* He knew not what to tell William. *Gone for help but never returned.* He had better have a good excuse for his failure to bring aid.

He could not spend this gold here. He would have to leave, get away as far as he could. Providence would not do, neither would Boston or New York. *Perhaps Jamestown?* he wondered.

Curtis thought once more of Mary, how she had placed the coins to her eyes. He did so now, drawing a pair from the chest and holding them just the same as she. Visions instantly swam as millions of lifetimes flashed through his mind. He watched fortunes be made and life savings lost, necks hanged from nooses and others adorned with jewels. He saw pirates opening chests filled with riches, and he saw among them William.

Curtis dropped the coins, dizzy from the experience and confused by the appearance of his friend.

Trying once more, he placed the coins and watched as cities replaced farmland, with buildings rising toward the sky. Carriages became horseless, faster than anything he had ever dreamed possible. Soon strange crafts flew across the sky, and some lives walked upon the moon.

A knock at the door interrupted his journey.

He dropped the coins into the chest and shoved it into the closet, hurrying to the window to look out.

"Curtis!" a voice shouted from outside, "It's me, William!" Soon, more knocking shook the room.

Curtis breathed deeply, unsure if he was ready to face his friend, not after the visions he had seen. But it *was* only William Mayes, his friend, the son of the tavern keep, not the pirate aboard a vessel called *Pearl*. He turned the knob and welcomed his friend inside.

"Judas, Curtis!" the man exclaimed, covering his nose at once. "You smell like you slept with swine!"

"I had a long night," was all Curtis Charles could say, afraid to mention too much. "Where did you go? How come you never returned?"

"What did you see after I left?" William demanded, ignoring the questions.

"I saw some things, not a lot," Curtis lied. "But they're witches for sure."

"I knew it!"

"You left me on my own, William. Why?"

"I had to. I ran into some friends and they... well, they had other plans for my night."

"I don't understand," Curtis frowned. Then he remembered what Mary had said about her farm being aflame. That image matched one he had seen of William just before he arrived. "*You* burned her farm!" he said. "With *my* torch and she'll blame *me*!"

"How did you..." William's face abruptly changed, filled with anger or fear. "Aye, I burned it, that's the only way to deal with witches."

"You said you were bringing help!"

"I did," replied William, and the door slammed open abruptly.

A stranger with a hard face chiseled with anger stepped forward. "And here they are now!" He was tall, darkly tanned, and slight of build. He looked to be about forty years old and was dressed elegantly, with golden lace adorning his blue jacket. His white linen trousers ended at the knee and embroidered stockings led into his boots. He wore a jewel-handled dagger and a golden chain around his neck. He was a man of danger and remarkable wealth.

Ann Mason also stood in the doorway, damp as if she had swum in her clothing, just behind the stranger.

"Enough pleasantries," the newcomer growled. "Does he have it or not?"

"I was working up to that, Thomas!" William replied angrily. "I asked you to wait."

"I wait for no man. The call to sea and lure of wealth is too great to resist," the man called Thomas barked. "Let's finish here and get back to the Pirate's Round!"

Thomas, Curtis mused taking the newcomer in. *Thomas Tew?*

William suddenly rounded on Curtis, striking his jaw with a balled fist. Unsuspecting, the latter fell to the floor.

"What did you see?" he demanded. "Did they reveal the whereabouts of the coins?"

"Wuh... what coins?" Curtis played dumb.

"He has 'em then," William decided, kicking his friend several times on the floor. "Where'd you stash 'em?"

"Wasted energy," Ann proclaimed, pushing her way into the room. "He's only got *one place* to hide 'em!" She opened the closet door and all eyes fell upon the chest, uncovered, and hastily pushed behind the door.

"Great mother of fortune!" Thomas Tew exclaimed, falling to his knees and flipping open the lid. He rejoiced at the find, a fortune of gold coins he scooped up and kissed. "It's them! John Dee's cursed treasure!" He turned to William. "This *is* enough payment, William Mayes, enough to earn your spot on my crew!"

"So the honor's mine? Officer's title without strings?" William demanded.

"Aye. Full and without strings. You can keep some of the gold we recovered last night, as well. Consider it an investment in your future."

"Thank you, Captain. When do we leave for the Arabian Sea?"

"Tonight," Tew said with a smile. "I've got what I came for, and now it's time to plunder the Mughal Convoy!"

"That's mine," Curtis said, surprising himself with his boldness. "You won't be leaving with it."

William's kick took him in the ribs, shattering two. "We take what we want, coward. And you *won't* follow, and do you know why?" He feigned crying and rubbed his eyes. "Because you're a sniveling son of a ferryman, a washed-up, terrified child afraid of the sea."

"Ah," said Tew, "don't treat the child so!" He walked over and tossed two coins on the floor beside Curtis. "Here's your share of the treasure, boy. Two coins. Two. That's all you get from Thomas *Tew*!" He roared laughter and joined William in breaking more ribs and bruising Curtis's skin.

Curtis languished as they beat him, his entire fortune gone in an instant. At some point he passed out, exhausted by the blunt trauma, but awoke once more. It was hours later, and he found himself crippled and bleeding in his own bed. He rolled over. Next to his face he found the coins left by Tew. A sorry wretch with no wealth but these, he reached out, desperate to know the future they now told, and placed them to his eyes.

A different fate unfolded before him, the fate of a man, tied to the sea, and leading men on a journey across the ocean. He recognized Captain Tew and watched as he met a horrifying death. Curtis laughed, emboldened by the man's untimely demise, and filled with hope for how this would all end.

Exhausted, he passed out once more.

Curtis awoke to darkness; night had fallen hours before and only pale moonlight entered his room. He groaned, the pain in his ribs overwhelming, and rolled over to relieve the pressure. As soon as he did, something slid off his face onto the bed beside him. His eyes shot open with remembrance and stared down at two coins.

Suddenly fearful, he felt inside his purse, finding Mary Griggs' resting safely there. Relieved, he looked up but soon gasped with shock. Against the wall leaned a torch, long extinguished and blackened by fire.

Why did William return this? he wondered, reaching the torch. But the answer was clear. It was returned as evidence in case the Constable investigated arson at Castle Hill. Two objects reflected light at its base, and he pulled himself off the bed and across the floor to investigate.

He held his breath, scooping a pair of golden discs into his hand, then held them up to the moonlight for a better look. The laughing skulls mocked him, laughing at his misery and especially the ignorance. He placed them over his eyes like the others, expecting a journey into the future. The rushing experience told another tale, one of desperation and mistakes made and for which the witches would pay.

He dropped the coins into the purse with the others, laughing and cackling like a mad man, unable to control his maniacal outburst.

Mary, he thought, *and Elizabeth.* Two witches with power, but not over him. Then he reached out and grabbed the torch, the mistake he himself had made by giving it over to William. Though cool, it burned in his hand but he could not let go, only an object, but suddenly an extension of his being.

Curtis felt the hex, a darkness that shivered his spine and sent spikes of fear through his chest. It made stronger the sensation of being lost, pulled to a place he did not belong. The coins he possessed burned as he recalled fates witnessed in each set, and cried out with pain as damnation rushed to his soul. But he would have the last laugh. A payment had been made by several, and each of them would further pay.

CHAPTER FOUR

The night air stilled over Newport, oddly stale and lacking the customary chill of the season. It had no smell and, like a bowl of unseasoned porridge one has to force down, it felt eerie to breathe in. The stars shone overhead, but the night birds did not sing and insects did not play their nightly orchestra. The entire island felt off.

Curtis made his way to the White Horse, hoping for a word with Ann Mason. She knew of witches and may also know a way to rid him of the curse. As he approached the tavern he noticed several more oddities. Though the tavern windows were lit, the building lacked its customary revelry and no one danced or moved around inside. Not a single horse was tied up out front, and no drunks staggered either in or out of its doors.

He pushed on the door and it swung easily, opening to a solemn display. Ann was alone in the building, sweeping up and clearing off tables.

"Where is everyone?" Curtis asked, causing the woman to startle.

"You just missed the rush. Don't you know the hour? Dawn will break soon."

"I only recently awoke," he replied. "Your friends did a number on me and might have left me for dead. I care not for the hour, only for a word with you."

37

"I've nothing *for* you. Tew is gone and so is William, left on the tide and making the Round. It'll be months or years before they return, if they do at all."

Curtis pulled out a chair and plopped down with a sigh, feeling at his ribs. Though sore, the pain was more of a dull ache to match the pounding in his head. "Do you have any food?" he asked.

Ann let out a laugh. "After what happened this morning, you come to me and ask for food? What if it be poisoned?"

"At this point, I no longer care. I'm famished, feel dead already, and don't care about the treasure they stole." A thought struck him. "What did *you* get out of it? What did Tew leave for you?"

"You mean, what did the captain pay me for all the time we spent tumbling between the sheets? Same as you," she replied scornfully, "only his *Tew* cents."

"I see. So how about that meal?"

"We've got some stew in the back," she suggested, setting her rag on the bar and carrying off two handfuls of mugs. "I'll be right back." She returned with a clean one, filled with ale and carrying a bowl and spoon.

Curtis frowned. She could have at least warmed the food, it arrived ice cold.

"Your girlfriend and I spoke today. She asked about Rose Sadler and demanded to know what she told me about them."

"She was right about them. They're witches, both," he replied, sniffing the stew and frowning at its lack of smell.

"She made that known to me as well, threatening curses and the like. But I didn't speak, gave nothing away at all. I'm loyal to my friends, see? Offered 'em a trade, even though Tew would never give up their precious gold, not even for those odd coins. That thought's amusing, isn't it? Knowing they hid away that wealth for decades but will never enjoy it? Let them look and wonder where it went, I say. It's lost to them till judgement day damns them to hell and their dark lord tells them himself!" She let out a chuckle. "Serves them both right, the evil bitches."

Curtis brought a spoonful of stew to his mouth, chewing it slowly. Along with aroma it also lacked flavor. He forced it down and sent a chaser of ale. It too proved flat, stale, and without even a hint of buzzing his pain. His stomach rumbled at the arrival of his meal, suddenly queasy. He lost interest in eating and pushed aside the bowl and mug.

"You should go now," Ann suggested. "I want to close up and get some rest."

Curtis rose and moved toward the door, pausing as he turned to ask one more question. "This *Tew* cents. Was it the same he paid me? Two of those strange coins?"

She nodded, scooping up his uneaten dinner and full mug of ale. "Aye, worthless ones at that."

"I'd keep them on you. They may come in handy later," he said, then stepped outside into the night. He found it the same as when he left it, bland and dull as the food and drink inside.

The waterfront beckoned and he made his way there, unsure what he would find. This time he found he no longer wished to run away, and remembrances of his father's death no longer caused him to fear the water. It seemed to beckon, waving him over, and he did, peering down into its murkiness.

Most of the ships had gone, now that Tew and his fleet had departed, and only a few merchants had moved closer to the town to fill his empty berths—even with him gone they were afraid. Curtis found it odd to find one small vessel tied off nearest the pier.

It was a ferry, one of those like his father piloted years before. The ferryman sat with his back to him, draped in a hood and staring off into the bay.

"Which ferry is this?" Curtis asked politely.

"Bristol," the pilot said without looking up.

"I've no need to go there," Curtis asked, "but it's been many years since I've ridden the bay in one of these. Would you take me as far as the break and bring me back? I can pay."

"That's not how a ferry works," the ferryman said dryly. "You must have a destination to ride, always a one-way trip."

Curtis dug into this purse, pulling out the two coins left by Tew and offering them with arm outstretched. "Please, sir. It would mean so much."

"Put your coins away, son. You should never pay the ferryman until you've reached the other side."

Defeated, Curtis returned them to his purse and turned to leave.

"I will make this exception once," the pilot offered, "and take you to the break and back."

The young man turned, suddenly eager to go out on the water as he once did with his father. He scrambled aboard and took a seat, excited to get underway.

"Toss that line, boy," the ferryman said, setting his oars. Curtis did and the boat slowly drifted into the harbor. Other than the splashing, there was no sound to the night, and Curtis watched the man labor.

"Won't you set the sail?" he asked after the man had rowed several hundred yards.

"With what wind?" the ferryman asked. "If you find some tell me from whence it blows, and I'll turn us into it." The laugh that followed was low and rumbly, stirring forth a memory in Curtis's mind. He had heard this laugh before, though he could not remember where.

"Why did you choose this line of work?" the young man asked.

"A ferryman does not choose his fate, just as he does not choose his fares."

"My father used to say that," Curtis said thoughtfully, wishing he could remember all the advice his father had given over the years. There had been so much of it.

"Do you know how to check draft?" the ferryman asked.

"I do. I used to do that for my father. He was also a boatsman." He leaned over the side, straining his eyes to see in the moonlight, but could not make out the markings.

"Here," the pilot said, holding out a darkened torch handle. As soon as Curtis grabbed it, the tip of it burst into flame, lighting the craft but not the boatman's face. It was still hidden behind his hood. "Every ferryman needs a torch. It does more than light the way. It can signal the shore and other boats or identify hazards in the water."

Curtis nodded, leaning over the side and holding it low by the water. Finding the draft lines much easier to read, he called them out. Just as he was turning to return the torch to its master, he paused, frowned, then held it out over the water.

"What's wrong?" the ferryman asked, amusement creeping into his voice.

"I thought I saw something." And he had. Two eyes staring up from beneath the surface. He held the torch lower, so low it sizzled by the spray of the oars. All at once twenty faces clamored upward, screaming silently beneath the water. One of them, he recognized, belonged to Mary Griggs. His first reaction was to reach out and help her, but then skeletal hands reached out for him, clawing at the side of the boat and scraping long nails against its hull. Curtis screamed, falling into the boat.

In his panic the torch fell, extinguishing as soon as it landed.

Again, the ferryman laughed.

"Who are they?" Curtis demanded. "*What* are they?"

"Souls, son," the ferryman explained. "The damned lost in their own misery, cursed to drown for one hundred years before I can help them."

Curtis wanted off the boat, straining his eyes in the moonlight to see the distant shore. On the beach thousands of figures ambled, stranded on water's edge and reaching desperate hands outward toward the bay. Their mournful cries begged for the ferryman to turn back, to fetch them and carry them across.

"Who are you," the boy pressed, "that the dead call out to you!"

The ferryman turned, picking up his torch with one hand and pulled back his hood with the other. Abruptly the torch sprang with life, lit aflame and illuminating a familiar face.

"No," Curtis begged, looking into his own countenance now gaunt with death and decay. Where his own eyes had once laughed with blue, two coins marked with laughing skulls stared back. He scrambled with fear, forgetting the size of the vessel, and fell over the side with a splash.

Arms wrapped around him immediately and sharp fingernails clawed at his flesh as he drifted down into the water. He held his breath as long as he could, desperate to cling to what was so plentiful above. Just before he let it go, another face swam into view. Curtis looked upon his father and screamed. His next gasp welcomed death.

CHAPTER FIVE

Curtis Charles gasped, breathing in air instead of water and confusing the two. In his mind he had drowned, but in reality he merely sputtered and spit while awakening. The confusion angered and consoled him at the same time. Living not dead, but neither life nor death no longer seemed better than the other.

He awoke in his own bed, beaten, bruised, and broken. Daylight reigned, illuminating his senses where he had once only seen darkness. A glance out the window brought instant regret as the light of day overwhelmed him. Falling against the wall, the young man covered his eyes and rocked against pain. He sat there for nearly thirty minutes before able to tolerate opening them even slightly.

After a while he stood with eyes clenched and made for his chest of drawers, tripping over some object on the floor. He soon regained his balance. With eyes tightly closed he never saw the object, but it was big so it must have been an overturned chair tipped over during his nightmare. He felt around, determined to go outside, and drew out one of his two other shirt—he only owned three—tying it around his head like a scarf and making sure it draped over his eyes. Only then did he stand, venturing out to face the day.

The stench of the street forced him back inside, an olfactory frenzy of horse manure, human feces, garbage, and rancid meat from the butcher shop next door. He swallowed back vomit, holding his breath while his sensitive eyes watered, then stepped out once more. Curtis hurried to the White Horse Tavern, intent on speaking with Ann Mason once more.

The sounds on the street harried him worse than the smell, as carters snapped whips at their horses, people conversed, and vendors cried their wares. His ears ached from the loudness, amplified by the pounding of his own feet as he ran.

The tavern was alive with its usual bustle, and early morning patrons argued over breakfast and gambling losses from the night before. With a deep breath he pushed open the door and, not wishing to draw attention, Curtis removed his head covering and made his way to the bar.

William's father was there, wiping up a spill and grumbling about the lack of help.

"Mr. Mayes," Curtis began, "have you seen Ann?"

"I haven't seen *her* nor my good for nothin' son!" the owner's voice boomed. Normally a softspoken man, his words caused Curtis to flinch. "He left in the night, boarded a ship with the Thomas Tew. He's gone back to piratin' that boy!"

The man's eyes narrowed, focused on Curtis's. "Do you even have your wits about you? The blacks of your eyes are huge, like there's no color in them at all."

"I'm sober, sir," the young man insisted. "I've had neither drop nor snuff!"

"Hmm," the tavern keeper doubted and returned to wiping the bar. "He left a letter before he left, my William. He said he'd be gone several years and said a few things about *you*, as well."

"What did he say, sir?"

William Mayes narrowed his eyes, appraising Curtis. "I don't think you're the bad sort," he finally said, then added, "but the constable's looking for you. Farmer Griggs claims you burned his farm, and now you're a wanted man."

"What did William say, sir? In his letter to you?"

"He said to stay clear of you, that trouble surrounds you!"

Curtis froze, his stomach rumbling from hunger so intense it nearly doubled him over. He stared at the tavern owner, remembering Mary's vision. *William had my torch,* he realized, *and they saw me carrying it earlier in the night!* He finally said, "I was nowhere near their farm, Mr. Mayes. Do *you* think I'm guilty?" he asked.

"Actually, my William *did* speak your praises, claiming you had nothing to do with the fire no matter what evidence they conjure... his words exactly."

Conjure... the word dripped with insinuations. *Was William warning of witchcraft? Mary and Elizabeth,* he reasoned, *what do they believe?*

From across the room a patron demanded a refill of ale, and the tavern keeper threw his rag down in frustration.

As Mr. Mayes turned to leave, Curtis asked one more time. "Where's Ann Mason?" he demanded. "I saw her here last night."

The older man froze in his tracks. "You say you saw her here? In the White Horse? What time would that have been?"

"I don't know. It was very late, but yes. I saw her and we spoke. To be honest, sir, she told me about William running off."

"That's impossible. I closed down the tavern myself. I had no help, so I drove out the patrons shortly after dinner. Only I have a key to that door, and I locked it tight when I left! Wherever you spoke to her wasn't here."

"She was here, sir, cleaning up! I swear!"

Mr. Mayes grunted, then attended his patron.

Curtis, with belly still empty, took a deep breath to steady his nerves before stepping out into the brightness. Blinding once again, he squeezed his eyes shut and tied the cloth over his head.

Where do I go now? He pondered, his feet carrying him out of town toward Castle Hills. *I could confront Mary, tell her what I saw, and that I had nothing to do with her farm.* But would that knowledge, that her secret was known, be enough she would accept him as a bride? *She's a witch!* he argued against himself.

Do I even want *to be married to a woman like that?* But Margaret Murphy had been one, and her husband loved her still, a widower forced to watch her flesh rendered ash by the stake. *Perhaps her dark dealings will mean nothing as a wife, merely a pastime she practices after dark.*

Then he remembered Farmer Griggs, a hulk of a man, strong and full of fight, rendered a slave to Elizabeth. When Curtis had seen him in the cave, the man appeared incapable of his own thought, a shell controlled by the coven.

Strong hands abruptly grabbed Curtis from both sides, forcing his hands behind his back. A gruff voice addressed him. "Hiding your face so we won't recognize you on the streets, Curtis Charles?"

"No!" he argued. "I... Who are you?"

"Take it off," the voice demanded, and the cloth was ripped away at once.

Curtis screamed with pain as light flooded his eyes, wailing and pulling away. His action, though involuntary, was met with fists to the ribs and a knee to the groin. He doubled over, defenseless and at these men's mercy.

"You are under arrest," the voice explained, "for arson."

"I've never..."

"We've testimony..."

"But no witness," the young man cried.

"Of that," the voice he now recognized as Constable Finneas Cooke explained, "we've no need!"

"I wasn't there!" Curtis cried out. "I was hiding, in the cave, when the Griggs' women worked their ritual! I saw it all, their witchcraft!" He sobbed, writhing against the light burning his pupils, and wept tears of blood. "Elizabeth and Mary Griggs are witches!" he accused. "I saw it all! I saw their entire coven!"

By now a large gathering had lined the streets, curious by the young man's accusations, and eager to see a show.

But the constable had other plans. He silenced Curtis Charles with a hand across his mouth. After he calmed, Cooke demanded, "Where is she?"

"Who?" Curtis pleaded.

"Ann Mason. What did you do with her?"

"Nuh... nothing! I saw her! Just last night we talked! She told me about William, that he sailed away with pirates! With Captain Thomas Tew!"

The constable frowned, rubbing his chin. "You admit you *saw* her? As early as last night?"

"I did! I swear I did!"

"Well then," the lawman said with a smile, "you wouldn't mind taking us to *your* place to prove you've nothing to do with her disappearance?"

"Not at all!" Curtis cried, his eyes burning from the daylight. Strong hands heaved him up and turned him in the street. Though the brightness overwhelmed him, he was aware of the gathering following as the constable pushed him toward the docks. The son of the ferryman made his way home mostly by instinct and fumbled as his key trembled before the lock.

"What's wrong?" the constable demanded. "Do you have something to hide?"

"Not at all!" Curtis insisted, pushing the heavy oak aside. "I'm innocent. My room is just as I left it!" As the door opened, he waved for the constable and him men to enter.

The refusal of the constable to move suddenly worried Curtis, as he focused his eyes to see what had frozen him in place. His bed was there, and so was his simple chest of drawers—pieces of furniture found in most every apartment of this time. His sheets were askew, and so was the blanket he used to keep warm, but also were the lines drawn on the floor. Unsteady, as if drawn in haste, they comprised a five-pointed star—a pentagram, just as the symbol Curtis first witnessed in the cave. In the center lay Ann Mason. Her lifeless eyes stared upward as if searching for a way home to the living.

How, Curtis wondered, *when?* Then he remembered his stumble... the object on the floor over which he tripped. *She was here,* he realized, *when I awoke and before venturing out. Only, I never saw her because I struggled to open my eyes!* Everything was lost in that moment, and he desperately tried to bargain. "Elizabeth and Mary Griggs are witches," he accused. "They did this," the young man insisted, "not I!"

"Oh really?" the constable asked. "Are you also going to suggest they burned down their own farm?"

"No! That was William Mayes and Thomas Tew!"

The two men with the lawman laughed, but the constable did not. "I've talked with Elizabeth Griggs, and she says you visited her place drunk with a torch in hand. She also says you left there, upset young Mary did not wish to be called upon." The man looked around, easily spotting the torch leaning against the corner. "Clamp him in irons," he told the men. "I'm taking him in for arson, murder, *and* witchcraft!"

Curtis resisted, struggling against their hold and what would come. "No! You don't understand!" he pleaded. "*They* are the witches! *They* did this! I saw them in a cave beneath the ..." As shackles locked around his wrists and ankles, a fist crashed bare knuckles against his mouth. Blood sprayed and a tooth loosened as his next words were cut off.

"Silence," the constable ordered, "I'll hear no more about this!"

They dragged him, limp and weak, all the way to the jail. Without concern for his head or body, they shoved him into the cell. The ground felt so cold, colder than it should, and Curtis felt bloody drool slip down his lip onto the stones. The crimson seemed so much more vivid than it should, scarlet instead of dull.

"Lock him in," the constable said to the others, "then leave the keys where some concerned citizen could easily find them, out on the desk, maybe. Then leave early, boys, tie one on at the White Horse, or go on home, it makes no matter to me. Just make sure no one's on duty at midnight."

The heavy iron bars slammed shut, and Curtis Charles blacked out once again.

CHAPTER SIX

Outside the barred windows the clock above town hall begin to chime. Almost immediately, the cuckoo above the constable's desk poked his head out and screamed his awful announcement that midnight had arrived. The deputies had kept their promise to the lawman and had departed several minutes before the cacophony. It was all orchestrated too well, and Curtis knew what to expect.

The door to the jail creaked open, revealing a large man with murder reflected in his eyes. Just beyond him, standing in the street with torches and angry chants, a mob had gathered.

"I didn't do it, Farmer Griggs," Curtis managed to say. "I swear I didn't burn your farm."

The burly man held up a torch, the same one left behind at his farm and, most recently, Curtis's own apartment. "Perhaps, but you accused my family of witchcraft, a lie you'll most certainly pay for."

Curtis protested. "I've guh... got no muh... money!" he explained, stammering like a man without wits. "Thomas Tew took it all, so what will I pay you with?"

"Your life," Josiah suggested.

Curtis felt his pocket, surprised his purse was still there. It held six coins now. He counted in his mind, the pair from the water, the two from Tew, and those found near the torch. Perhaps he could use these to bargain? But he knew better, they were worthless for barter, except to men like Thomas Tew.

Farmer Griggs pressed an iron key into the cell door and turned. The gate swung open with a click.

Curtis opened his mouth to barter the coins, but whatever words he uttered left his body in a rush of breath. The unlit torch, the bane of Curtis Charles' past few days, swung downward and collided with his spine. The ribs broken the morning before cracked wider with a fresh jolt of pain.

The farmer leaned down, close enough Curtis could smell the false courage on his breath, and whispered, "Mary told me also to find these and slide them into your pocket. "They're the pair she dropped in the water." Two coins found their way against the young man's breast. "She said to tell you it's for passage."

"And the others? Those planted in my room with that torch?" Curtis demanded, suddenly angry and defiant.

Josiah pulled a pouch from his pocket, one meant to be worn around a neck. "Those belonged to Elizabeth. She said they won't work, now you cursed and gave them to Tew. She sends the same message, that they're for passage."

Curtis's eyes came into focus, staring at the Christian crowd beyond the door. Their curses and chants were no better than the witches' he'd witnessed, and he silently damned them all to hell. "I've done nothing to harm you at all, Mr. Griggs, so, when you kill me, it'll be your own damnation you ensure."

Strong hands heaved the young man up, and the farmer proclaimed, "I make my weekly donation and take communion when it's offered. I'm certain about *my* fate. Make right with your *dark* lord, so he knows you're on the way down to him."

Curtis, suddenly no longer caring what happened to neither himself nor his soul, spit in the farmer's eye and laughed.

A solid fist collided with his skull, and Curtis Charles blacked out one more time.

The cackling sound was pleasant, soothing even, and lured him deeper into slumber, but the searing heat upon his ankles forced Curtis's eyes open. The crowd chanted as he burned, damning him to hell and decrying all others like him.

If they only knew the real witches walked among them, he thought. The fire had grown, but death would be slow. No accelerant had been used, at least none he could smell.

A figure approached, stepping up onto a stool and reaching over the flames into his pocket. "These are your payment, Curtis Charles," Mary whispered into his ear. "You'll become something different now, and I give them to you freely. In return, I want a different future than I saw."

"I would have loved you," he managed through clenched teeth, the pain unlike any he'd ever felt.

"It would have been unrequited," she assured him, placing the coins to his eyes and pressing just a bit too hard with her thumbs. "Look," she whispered, "into the future and find your fate."

Curtis did, just as he had so many times over recent days. But this time the fate he witnessed was not buried deep under so many others. Each time before when he gazed, he saw his friend, his acquaintances—even perfect strangers. But this time, he only saw one pathway. The flames would claim him, his heart stopping from the pain before the hairs on his head had even singed, but this vision did not end there.

Curtis Charles would die, but a part of him—call it even his soul—would live on. He laughed, the sound no longer like a madman, but of victory. "Oh, Mary," he said loud enough the mob hushed. "Don't you see what you've done? You and Elizabeth are cursed by your own mistake! A *grave* one, certain to haunt you forever. I see my fate, sure, but it far out-reaches your own!"

"Shut up," the girl hissed, pressing the coins harder into his eyes.

"That's just it! I can't stop! I've seen my fate, lived it already, and there's *nothing* left for me to fear! These coins you show me, I've already seen," he said. "Yours are in my pocket, and these I left for you to find! You show my own fate I have already seen!"

"Step back, Mary!" her father commanded. "His curses will damn you even if the flames only catch your hem!"

But the girl did not listen. She leaned in closer, full of rage and fury, hellbent on changing the course of her own destiny.

"Take back what I saw!" she demanded. "Change my fate, at least the part regarding *you*!" The fact Curtis did not cry out forced her fingers and the coins deeper into his skull, tokens now of deeper meaning than what her mother once intended.

"I need only two," Curtis said calmly, just as the jelly within his orbs ruptured. He flinched at that, but continued. "The curse demanded you pay me passage. Two coins to carry you upon your way, but you paid the wrong amount."

"Right amount," Mary insisted, driving the gold deep into his skull, "two coins for the Ferryman!"

"Only you haven't paid me two," Curtis explained. "You paid me three while your mother paid me one!"

"You are a liar and a drunk! I *hate* you, Curtis Charles! I will not live the fate I saw!"

"You will," the dying man whispered, "because you paid me before your journey even began."

The girl fell back, but Curtis could not see her tumble. His eyes were gone, replaced by two of the coins Mary paid for passage. In his pocket lay two different coins, safely stashed with others, and through these he witnessed her fate as clearly as she had. This girl was destined for insanity and would forever drown in a sea of souls.

Meanwhile, Curtis Charles died. In his place only the Ferryman remained.

PART II
THE RITUAL

CHAPTER SEVEN

Castle Hills, Rhode Island Colony, Two Days Earlier

Mary Griggs hummed as she worked, happy and seemingly walking on air with her head lost in the clouds of imagination. Curtis Charles, the young man from Newport, had asked for her hand.

He had no wealth, of course, but he was so kind and thoughtful. The first time they had met he offered to unload Father's wagon, earning *his* respect and, if not admiration, a bit of tolerance for potentially hanging around the farmer's daughter. That was a feat of its own, as Josiah Griggs never trusted any boy or young man around Mary. Large in stature and cursed with an angry brow, he had always chased away her suitors with only a glare. Toward her and Mother, of course, Father was as gentle as a newly birthed foal.

Mother had liked Curtis right off, seeming not to care about his empty pockets or lack of prospects. He worked as a laborer, working odd jobs here and there as a mason, a carpenter, and sometimes a smith. But he was never found working around the docks. Mary had noticed early on how he avoided work as a fisherman or even a ferryman like his own father before. She had asked him about that aversion, his resentment toward the sea, and he answered truthfully. The ocean had claimed his father and nearly him.

Mary Griggs liked this young man and could not remove him from her thoughts no matter how hard she tried.

"The sun has barely risen, and already you've forgotten your senses," Mother said from across the pen. "You're wasting grain, spreading much of it where the chickens can't reach." Elizabeth Griggs was a beautiful woman, still youthful though past child-bearing prime. Only a bit of gray tinted her auburn locks, a trait passed down to her daughter. She and Mary were nearly identical in every way except age and seemed, in this moment, to even share a thought. "Can you put off thinking of this boy until after breakfast, at least?"

"I can't help it. I think I'm in love. He even asked me for his hand."

This brought a smile to Elizabeth's face. She had never heard her daughter profess even a hint of being ready for marriage, but her eyes betrayed worry.

"What is it, Mother? Father likes him, and Curtis Charles would make a wonderful farmer. He can do everything Pa does, from mending hearth and fence to building tools and fixing those which broke. He's strong, not as strong as Father of course, but strong enough to steer a plow."

"True," Elizabeth agreed, "He's all of these things, but I'm worried about our family's legacy." She waved her hand, pointing out the entire farm. "This belonged to *my* father, and he scrutinized everyone who called upon me. This place comes with a secret, Mary, one which I only shared with your father *after* we had been married a full year."

Mary paused, considering, and looking around the farm. It had always been a simple spread, perched high upon Castle Hill, and very near the lighthouse pointing out the rocks below. Though sizable, it was nothing like the larger plantations in Providence and Plymouth. "Secrets?" she asked, full of confusion. "Like what, Mother? What secrets could *we* have?"

"The lighthouse, for one," Elizabeth admitted. "The keeper does not own it nor the property upon which it stands. That all belongs to us, bought and paid for by my grandfather. The keeper is paid a stipend managed by Newport and some of the other townships, and they also pay upkeep on the structure. But we own it all down to the rocks below. Grandfather Seamus Flannigan built the original and also our house and barn."

"Well," Mary exclaimed, that truly *was* a secret that spoke of some past family wealth. "If Grandfather Flannigan was so rich to have built a lighthouse and owned all of Castle Hill, why aren't we the richest family in Rhode Island?"

Elizabeth's brow frowned deeper and her smile disappeared. "That's just it, Mary, that's the secret. We *are* the richest family in Rhode Island."

Mary laughed hysterically, scaring the chickens and sending them clucking away from their feed. She raised the hem of her stained dress, indicating where it had been torn and restitched over the years and laughed even more. Though well fed and healthy, the Griggs family was *anything* but wealthy.

"Did I miss something?" she demanded, looking around and unable to control the remnants of humor in her voice. "Or am I missing the butler, maids, and other servants?" She scrambled over the fence and ran to the pigpen, bowing deeply before the mud covered beasts within. "Will Duke and Lady Porker be staying with us long, Mum?" she asked without holding back her sarcasm.

Turning, she found Elizabeth staring back unamused. Her mother dumped the pile of grain she held in her hem and straightened her skirt. Then she wiped the dust from her hands. "Let's go for a walk," she said dryly, leading her daughter toward the lighthouse.

They walked in silence, with Mary brimming with curiosity and wonder. When they finally reached the rocks, she looked out over the bay and watched the sea crash into Hull Point on the other side. The water between the two points glistened with daylight as it rose high above. After several minutes, she broke the silence. "I see water, Mother. Water and rocks, not wealth."

"More wealth has crashed upon these rocks over the years than has grown in the tilled fields we own. There was a reason Grandfather Flannigan built this beacon, and it was to hide in plain sight his riches."

"I don't understand."

"Ever since Europeans found the Americas, they've been plundering its wealth and crashing it against rocks like these. That's what Grandfather Flannigan found when he settled here in 1636. He was fed up with Roger Williams, a rebellious young firebrand chased out of every other Puritan congregation."

"Great Grandfather split away from Providence? I thought he settled here directly," Mary pondered.

"He originally sailed with Williams, but secretly ventured out to find a plot of land to call his own. He found these rocks and, on this shore, a treasure hidden beneath centuries of debris. He gathered it all, piece of eight by piece of eight, until he amassed a fortune of gold and jewels."

"What did Roger Williams do? Why didn't he force him to settle near the township? Why didn't he force Grandfather to pay his share of taxes?"

"Because Grandfather was an intelligent man, a schemer with a wife both wise and crafty. Grandmother Molly hatched the plan after he showed her the treasure, and together they convinced Williams of the need for a lighthouse at Castle Point. He granted them Castle Hills as a homestead, as long as they promised to keep the lighthouse burning and journey to Providence once a month to attend his services—claimed they needed to remain part of his flock to live in his Rhode Island."

"So they hid it away? Never told him about the treasure?"

Elizabeth nodded, then turned quickly, leading her daughter toward their house. Mary had to hurry to catch up, straining to listen while also watching her steps on the rocks.

"Roger Williams was a greedy man," her mother said, "eager to line his pockets while growing his church. For that, he needed all the wealth Rhode Island had to offer. After him, if he had taken his unfair share, whatever was left would have been heavily taxed by King Charles, leaving nothing for Grandfather Flannigan and Molly."

"So they hid it?" Mary asked.

They had reached the house, and Elizabeth threw open the door to their root cellar. Rows of bins filled with sweet potatoes, garlics, and onions lined the wall, and jars of food filled the shelves above them. Far in the corner rested several wheels of cheese. Elizabeth knelt, rolling these aside and pressed against a panel.

"My bedroom is directly above us," she explained, "and we also have a hatch beneath our bed which can access what's behind this panel." With a twist and a pull, the panel came away revealing two chests beneath the floorboards of her chamber. She grabbed one, tugging it toward her, and lifted the lid.

Mary gasped at the riches, reflecting light from the open cellar door and whispering of the great opportunities so much wealth could offer. And this was only one chest. She looked up at her mother, surprised to find her smiling back at her daughter.

"This will all go to *you* someday, and to your husband, of course."

"There's so much," Mary whispered.

"Which is why we cannot reveal it all at once. To do so would bring down the governor and his tax collectors—possibly even magistrates and constables. They would rightfully claim our family hid it away, evading taxation and living in violation of the king's law."

"Can't we bribe them? There's enough here we could let some of it go if it meant changing our lifestyle!"

"No. An abrupt change would also draw attention." Elizabeth sighed. "So now you know our family's secret. We're cursed with wealth we can only spend but a bit at a time. We can't sell the jewels in town, and Spanish pieces of eight draw attention of their own no matter where we may try to rid ourselves of them. Once a year, your father goes into Boston and sells a bit of the least obvious trinkets there. He brings that coin back here, and we use it to expand the farm little by little. Eventually we will turn such a profit that no tax collector will wonder where our wealth comes from. Hopefully that will be in *your* lifetime."

"Mine and whichever husband I choose."

"Exactly," Elizabeth agreed. "And now you know why you must be choosy, selecting a man who will keep our secret and also live discreetly. Avoid the drunkards, they have a tendency to brag."

"I will, Mother," Mary promised, watching as Elizabeth closed the lid and returned the chest and the panel to their original state. "But how will I know who is my best suitor? It's not like I can magically divine my fate."

"Actually," Elizabeth explained, "we have a way to do exactly that. Grandmother Molly Flannigan was of the old ways, a Celtic mystic."

Mary gasped. Mysticism went against her Christian teachings. "Witchcraft?"

"Not at all," Elizabeth explained. "Mysticism is the opposite of witchcraft. It's about harmony with nature, a spiritual connection between God's creation and our inner soul. He placed us here, in this Garden of Eden, and we are tethered to both Heaven and Earth. Our ancestors learned to tread in both, and Celtic mysticism is about life and love, not darkness and evil. It's certainly *not* devil's work like witchcraft."

Mary could not believe her ears. If Pastor Jedediah heard these words, he would demand her mother be burned at the stake. "So Rose Sadler and the others, who made those accusations about you?"

"Were *real* witches, angry we did not share a like mind with them."

"We? I don't understand what you mean by *we*, Mother! I don't believe like you do!"

"You may, once you've seen what I can show you. No, I mean *we* as in your father, myself, and two other couples in Newport. They, like us, share ancestry rooted in mysticism."

"Father accepts this?" Mary stood, nearly hitting her head on the floorboards above. She felt so much confusion, eyeing the cellar door and the light pouring in.

I am the light, the bible teaches, *and whatever is done in darkness will be exposed!*

"Your father accepts this," Elizabeth insisted, "because his mother was a mystic also."

"I never believed any of this possible!" Mary felt her feet moving toward the light. She yearned for spiritual cleansing, to pick up her bible and run to the chapel, to seek absolution for her family's sins.

"When you are ready," her mother went on, "I will show you how to see your own fate. You will know, then, who you can and cannot trust as a husband and also may learn to accept our family's secrets as your own."

Those words were enough and sent Mary racing from the cellar and out into the light of day. She did not retrieve her bible, however, and did not race toward the church as she thought she should. Instead, Mary Griggs ran toward the lighthouse. She needed to think. She also needed to pray.

CHAPTER EIGHT

The sun set upon the Griggs' farm, cloaking it fully in darkness that forced a shudder down Mary's spine. As she peered out the window, her mother placed a supportive hand on her shoulder.

"You have chosen wisely," her mother promised, "and will gaze upon your fate tonight. Based on what you see, you will know which paths to choose and will have confidence in your choices."

"I'm afraid." Mary admitted. "Will it hurt?"

"No. Even if the ritual proves a harbinger of ill tidings, you will know which hazards to avoid on your journey through life. I saw flaws in mine, dark things I have managed to avoid altogether. As long as you follow the ritual exactly, you will not be damned to whatever you see."

"But there's a price?"

"There's always a price. The coins your father will bring to you are yours alone to keep. You must be the one to bear them after tonight, just as I carry mine." Elizabeth held up a pouch worn around her neck. "I keep them here, assurance of my passage to the underworld. They are trinkets, with no value in this world despite their golden composition. They cannot be melted down, and no coin collector will want them."

"So they're *cursed*?" Mary demanded.

"No. Grandmother Molly cleansed them of the curse they once held, one placed using witchcraft."

"What witch placed that curse?"

"A dark man, a *foul* pirate named Jean Le Sage. He was a Frenchman who sailed the Americas at a time the Spanish claimed it all. His ship, called *Drake*, was a thumb in the nose to Queen Elizabeth, herself. Named for Sir Francis, he stole it, aiming to push England into an all-out war, one that would chart a different fate for the New World."

"Where did he find the coins?"

"They belonged to the queen's astrologer, a Celtic mystic named John Dees, who would divine for her using the old ways. He minted the coins, stamping them with the image of the Ferryman."

"Do you mean Charon? Like in Greek mythology? He ferried the souls to the underworld."

"He is called Manann to our people, spoken of today in the Arthurian legends. Although, the place is now confused with the one who ferries souls across. Even King Arthur had to cross over to the island, a place originally known as Tech Duinn but is now called Avalon. As Christians, we call it Heaven."

"So Dees cursed the coins, not Le Sage?"

"No. Dees fashioned them in the old magic, as payment to Manann, or simply the Ferryman. Queen Elizabeth coveted control over all her destiny. Faced with a war against the Spanish, she had commissioned the minting of these coins to learn how to defeat their Armada and chart her empire's course in the New World. Sir Francis, who sailed with Dees, was the first to test them, divining his own fate and testing their efficacy. He, with his own pair against his breast, took the queen's to her aboard a faster vessel, *Golden Hind,* leaving *Drake* with Dees. He arrived in time, defeating the Spanish Armada for his queen."

"But Dees made more of the coins. Why?"

"An entire chest full, so that every king or queen of England would be masters over fate. He was bringing them to England from an island in the Caribbean when Le Sage attacked him and took both the coins and *Drake*."

"What did he do with them, these coins?"

"Once he realized their power, he set out to curse them, to deny the Ferryman of his treasure and make them so that whoever carries the coins can see through them without owing them to Manann as payment."

"But Molly cleansed them? So we again owe them to the Ferryman after we die?"

"Yes. Two coins are the price for passage, no more, no less."

"But I will know my future and be able to prolong my life by making decisions that put off death?"

"Yes. You will also know how to use our family's wealth and gain even more. There are so many possibilities once you have the knowledge."

Mary thought once more of Curtis Charles. *He's a kind man, a sweet man, and I truly hope he's the one for me. I want to know; I need to know my fate.* "I'll do it, Mother," she finally agreed. "I'll take part in the ritual and learn how to protect our family's treasure. But where do we find Dees' coins if they were stolen by Le Sage."

"Along with the treasure hidden beneath our home, Grandfather Flannigan also found the wreck of *Drake,* washed ashore at Castle Point, all hands lost to the sea."

Mary gasped. "What were they doing so far north of the Caribbean?"

"New France, called Nouvelle-France, a place we call Newfoundland. He had a base there, much as Thomas Tew does in Rhode Island today."

Mary shuddered at mention of the pirate, Thomas Tew. She had crossed his path once, when he visited town. She had passed in front of the White Horse Tavern on her way to pray in the chapel. When she laid eyes upon him, she feared she had seen the devil himself, licking his lips and fondling his own crotch as she passed. The way he had leered made her feel unclean, a lecherous demon she hoped to never run across again. *If I learn my fate, I will also know when to avoid this man as well.*

"I'm ready, Mother. I will do it. When do the others arrive?"

"We will meet them at the place around midnight, but we have much more to prepare between now and then."

"Prepare? Like what?"

"Like me," her father's deep voice rumbled. Josiah stood in the entrance of his bedroom, dressed in light linen as if it were summer and not autumn.

"Prepare you, how? *Why*? What role will *you* play?"

"I will be the one to gather your coins, but cannot touch them with my soul intact before passing them to you. If I do, then you will see my fate, not your own."

Mary looked toward Elizabeth for explanation. "Mother?" she asked. "What does he mean?"

"Your father must be a draugr, a husk void of both life and death and able to touch the coins without exacting payment. I will borrow his soul, storing it beside mine until safe to return it to his body."

"How will we do that?" Mary asked, suddenly very afraid.

"With this," Josiah said, as if holding up a live rabbit by its hind legs were explanation for everything. "Come, Elizabeth, we should do this now, before the others arrive. I don't want one of *them* stealing my soul by accident."

"I agree. Come," she beckoned for Mary to follow, "and I'll walk you through your first ritual."

The rabbit, it turned out much to Mary's relief, was not a sacrifice but a grounding element for her and her mother's combined energy. The pitiful looking hen, however, locked in a cage with a knife laying nearby, had a much different fate. Unlike when butchering a fowl for dinner, during the ritual this poor animal screamed. It writhed with pain, both physical and mental anguish, as it seemed to recognize its contribution to the night.

Mary felt ill, her stomach tying into knots as her mother knelt over Josiah with blood dripping from the severed head and neck. The chanting Elizabeth muttered added more apprehension, a mixture of trepidation and horrified realization that this entire event was no dream.

"Leithleach," Elizabeth commanded her husband, "Leithleach agus ardú!"

Josiah's body began to tremble, not like a seizure nor tremor from the cold, but a slight ripple that flowed through the softer flesh around his bones. Every piece of muscle, sinew, and skin quivered as if it were water made to ripple. In contrast, the rabbit sat unbothered nearby, perfectly content to be witness to the ritual.

"Leithleach agus ardú!" Elizabeth said again. "Rise and separate! Leave the body! An corp seo a thréigean!"

All at once, his muscles ceased moving. Even his chest no longer rose or fell, and Mary rushed to her father's side. Holding her ear to his chest, she listened, praying for him to breathe.

"You killed him!" she screamed at her mother, eyes filled with tears and so blinded she did not see the open palm striking her cheek.

"Don't lose your wits!" Elizabeth warned, the sternness of her words stinging more harshly than the slap.

Mary continued to watch her father's chest. With no breath or heartbeat detectable, he had certainly died. Her own heart raced. Panicked, she looked first toward her mother who continued to chant, unconcerned about her husband's death.

Then she noticed the rabbit. Like her father before, its skin and muscles beneath rippled as if moving at once. As if hind legs were grasped by an invisible force it suddenly arced in the air, slammed onto the ground a half-circle away. Its muscles rippled again, followed by another arc into the air and onto the floor. It happened once, twice, three times. After a brief pause it furiously flew more times than Mary could count.

This all proved too much for the girl, and she screamed frantically. This time, Elizabeth did not interfere, too entranced by chanting to raise a hand to either console or correct her daughter.

Josiah Griggs' eyes abruptly snapped open.

The rabbit immediately stopped seizing.

The body of the hen, once discarded on the floor, leapt to its feet and raced out the bedroom door.

"Catch it," Elizabeth commanded, and Mary scrambled into action, chasing the beheaded animal first into the living room, and then the kitchen. It turned around, dodging her attempted grasp, and sprinted toward the bedroom.

Mary struggled with her emotions. This would have been humorous had her father not nearly died just a few minutes earlier, and had she not witnessed the invisible hand torturing the rabbit. Choking down a sob, she managed to corner the dismembered fowl, scooping it up by a wing. It felt very much alive.

"Toss it into the fireplace," Elizabeth said calmly from the bedroom door. A soulless Josiah stood behind his wife—fully animated, but most certainly without life behind those vacant eyes.

As soon as fire touched the hen, it ceased movement, its feathers curling in the flame. The smell was sickening, reminding Mary of burnt hair. She turned to meet her mother's exhausted stare. "How," she demanded "was that *not* witchcraft?"

"I told you, witchcraft is darker and with a fouler purpose."

Something moved between Elizabeth's legs and both mother and daughter looked down. The hare hopped calmly toward the door as if hoping for release. Mary looked toward her mother who nodded, then opened the door to let it out. Not far down the lane a torch bobbed in the darkness, moving steadily toward their home.

"We have visitors," Mary exclaimed.

"At this hour?" Elizabeth joined her in looking out. "Who would make this walk in the dark?"

The torchlight lit up a face Mary recognized. "It's Curtis Charles," she gasped.

"Get rid of him," Elizabeth demanded. "I'll hide your father."

Mary waited, back against the door, breathless and hoping it wasn't obvious. Part of her, the fanciful girl, felt delight at the sight of her beau. But the timing, it wound her panic tighter, gripping her insides as if to wring them out.

A timid knock announced Curtis's arrival.

Mary immediately answered the door. "What are you doing here?" she asked the young men, trying very hard to hide the irritation behind her words.

"I had to see you, Mary, I..." Curtis began. His breath was horrible, doused heavily with drink.

Never trust a drunkard to keep our family secrets, Mary thought, remembering her mother's warning. *But I've never seen him this way, certainly this was only to build courage!* She placed a hand over her nose and mouth and proclaimed. "You smell like a brewery, Curtis Charles!"

"I had a few, Mary, but I'm not bad-off drunk. I walked most of it off." He leaned against the frame, his torch moving dangerously close to the thatch roof.

"Step away with that thing!" Mary abruptly cried, watching sparks sputter against the straw.

Curtis backed up immediately, ashamed of his clumsiness.

"Who's at the door, Mary?" Elizabeth asked, feigning ignorance.

Mary felt relief at her mother's help and called out, "Curtis Charles and William Mayes, Mother. But they're just leaving."

Her mother stepped into the entryway and addressed the boys. "If you've come calling on my daughter, you've done so at too late an hour, Curtis. You'll have to come back tomorrow."

"I'm sorry," he begged. "I heard some awful things in the tavern, rumors I thought you should hear from me."

Mary's eyes darted to meet her mother's which seemed to urge caution.

Elizabeth smiled at the boys and calmly answered, "Let me guess, Ann Mason has been spreading stories about us being witches? We've been down this path when Rose Sadler and Margaret Murphy were condemned. Both the constable and magistrate know we're devout Christians. They already tossed out those accusations. We appreciate your concern, but we're fine. Please go home and we'll talk again tomorrow."

"I'm sorry, Mrs. Griggs," Curtis begged, but Elizabeth shut the door between them.

Elizabeth addressed Mary at once. "Do you not see it now? The reason you must learn your fate?"

"Yes, Mother." Mary thought of Curtis's drunken state and how he carelessly held the torch.

"Good. I sent your father out the back door, to meet us at the gathering point. Watch from the window until you're certain those boys are gone, then we'll follow him to the waterfront."

Mary nodded, wishing this night had never happened, but silently praying Curtis Charles would play a major role in her fate.

She didn't have to wait long before the torch bobbed out of sight. It was time to learn her destiny.

CHAPTER NINE

Mary followed her mother to the ledge. She found it more difficult to find her way in the dark, but Elizabeth seemed to know the path by memory. It led to a spot she had never before known existed, much less imagined so close to their home. Nestled into rocks behind the lighthouse, a boulder had been moved aside. Further inspection revealed it to be a door, expertly camouflaged and well-hidden when closed. Beyond the opening a winding passage opened up before her, leading deep into the stone and again downward to sea level.

"Why have I never seen this passage, Mother?" she asked.

"It's another of our secrets, only a select few know of it. Grandfather Flannigan designed it when he constructed the first lighthouse." A deep moaning echoed upward, a man's voice, deep and in pain. "Hurry!" Elizabeth urged.

A woman's voice followed not long after the man's. "Eirigh suas!" women's voices proclaimed. "Eirigh suas! Eirigh suas!" she called.

"That's a call for healing!" Elizabeth exclaimed. "Finneas may be hurt!"

"Finneas?" Mary wondered. "Finneas Cooke, the constable?" She suddenly understood why the accusations against her mother had disappeared. With the constable on her side, no decent investigation would be made.

"Yes, he and Sally will be joining us. That sounds like them up ahead." As soon as she had spoken, the passage opened into a larger cavern. At the bottom of it lay an undisturbed pool nestled against a rock wall. Several torches lit the shoreline, and on the floor lay a man with two women standing over him. Each was cloaked in the same hooded robe as Elizabeth and Mary. One she recognized as Sally Cooke, the constable's wife, the other appeared to be Amelia Saunders, wife of Newport's magistrate. All in attendance were people of great consequence to the colony.

Sally Cooke turned to Elizabeth as soon as she arrived. "There was someone here when we arrived. He struck Finneas and pushed us aside as he ran by." She pointed a shaking finger at the middle of the room.

Mary turned her eyes from the injured man, now standing and in less pain than before. Beyond him, written in the sand, she spied a five pointed star written in blood. A dead goat lay in the middle, a cavity cut into its chest, and with lifeless eyes fixed on the pool. She screamed, a bloodcurdling sound that echoed through the chamber.

"Focus!" Elizabeth whispered, "and help us heal him!"

"Where's Father," Mary demanded.

"He'll join us soon," her mother explained, taking up chanting with the others. "Shíolraigh agus ardú," she sang out loudly.

The others responsed, "Eirigh suas!"

Mary joined in after the second recitation, marveling at how Finneas grew stronger with each.

As they chanted, the group moved to the water's edge. Mary watched as her mother frowned, drawing forth an object from the slain goat and holding it closer to a torch for inspection. Larger than expected from the small animal, both women realized at once it was a human heart, and Elizabeth squeezed it over the pool of water. Whatever dark art was performed, draining it dry would lessen its affect. "We must hurry," she whispered to the others.

"A dark ritual was done here tonight, and we must do this as soon as my husband arrives."

The others clamored frantically in hushed voices, each terrified by the intrusion. They all watched as the animated husk of Josiah emerged as a shadow swimming in the water, rising up and splashing his way to shore. He walked directly to Mary.

The girl stepped forward, careful not to step on the goat laying prostrate on the ground, standing just beside it and reaching eagerly for the coins. Her father pressed them into her palm, his eyes staring vacantly in the torchlight.

Elizabeth handed him a robe with which to cover his dripping form, then stepped behind her daughter. She whispered instructions. "Hold them to your eyes, daughter, and look through them. Repeat after me," she added. "Atropos, Clotho, and Lachesis! I am your servant, a slave to the fates and blind to your secrets."

"Atropos, Clotho, and Lachesis!" Mary recited, "I am your servant, a slave to the fates and blind to your secrets."

Elizabeth went on, her lips very close to her daughter's ears. "Reveal them now. Show unto me the lessons from Manann."

"Reveal them now," Mary said trembling. She was terrified, but so far the coins had remained only those. "Show unto me the lessons from Manann."

A vision slowly formed in the girl's mind. She marveled at it, a beautiful scene of the bay and her family's farm. Only, the buildings were different, rebuilt and modern, akin to those being built in Europe. From one of them, a beautifully painted three-story structure with a tall lookout and colonial porch, three children ran outside to play in the field.

"What do the fates show you, Daughter? Tell us, now, as you see!"

She suddenly gasped. "I see it, Mother! It's happening as you promised!"

But then she wondered, *Are these my children?* she watched as they spun around and chased each other about. A strong man worked near the barn, overseeing dozens of servants who hauled in a massive harvest of pumpkins and squash. The wealth she witnessed in this vision was overwhelming, and she smiled gleefully. Then she realized, the man she saw was *not* Curtis Charles, but she suddenly found herself yearning to be with *this* man, strong, and handsome, and powerfully rich.

A woman appeared on the porch then, and Mary realized something was wrong. This was not her fate; this was the fate of Castle Hill. *Show me mine!* she demanded. *Show me my fate instead!*

And then she saw herself, a woman, unmarried, living in a common house. Neither servant nor lady, she was dressed in a hospital gown and surrounded by attendants dressed all in white. The straps on the bed, held her tightly restrained.

"I... I do not marry, not Curtis Charles or *any* man! I'm a spinster! Someone else lives in a grand home at Castle Hills, but it isn't me. I'm... I'm in a different *kind* of home for those who've lost their wits!" Mary began to tremble, her fingers shaking as she held the coins to her eyes.

The image abruptly changed, suddenly nighttime. Starlight shown overhead and only a sliver of moon lit the ground beneath. Her house was as it was, simple and the place she knew as home. All around it dark figures scurried, hauling out valuables and carrying them off toward a wagon. On the front stoop a dark figure lit a torch, swinging it about before tossing onto the thatch roof.

"I see... fire! Flames as high as treetops! Oh, Mother, it's our home! Our house and barn burn as we speak! Our fortune is taken, stolen by he who started the fire!"

The flames extinguished at once, revealing a new figure standing just in front of her eyes. This man wore a black grave shroud, the kind the coroner would wrap around the body of a witch once burned. His flesh had burned away, leaving behind a skeletal figure with an accusing finger raised. His face a skull, his eyes stared back through the same coins she held in her hand.

"Calm, child," Elizabeth urged. "Since you've seen this fate there's time to prepare and change it. When does the fire occur?"

Damned to madness, the specter accused.

Show me my fate! she demanded. *What becomes of me?*

The figure laughed a throaty rasp as he faded away, replaced by a woman with shaven head. Ghostly scratches from fingernails once long and sharp were now ancient scars lining her scalp, telling a gruesome tale of turmoil and pain. Every laceration told a different story in Mary's mind, one of loss, regret, dashed hope, and self-loathing. The woman tried to scratch more of the same, but found she could not, rubbing the nubs of her fingertips as if she could. Someone, a doctor maybe, had removed those weapons against her fate, pulling them free each time they regrew.

The girl, with downturned head, cackled, sensing Mary watching. "I feel you watching," the woman said, laughing and turning vacant eyes upward. "Watching *me* while your farm burns!"

Her eyes... The reason her nails had been plucked? Where bright blue orbs once smiled at the world, Mary Griggs' eyes had been gouged in some gruesome act of self-mutilation. "They're there," the eyeless Mary told the younger version, pointing to a jar with bobbing objects floating around for a look of their own.

Mary broke from her trance, letting out a whimper and dropping the coins. They bounced and rolled on the rocks, one of them disappearing into the void and sending tiny ripples to disrupt the once again still waters. She slid to her knees and wailed mournfully. "Now, Mother! The fire burns *now!*"

Elizabeth hefted her daughter to her feet and pushed her toward the others. Noticing something shiny on the rocks, she instinctually stooped to pick it up. She stared down at the

Ferryman's coin, holding it up. It belonged to her daughter, and only she should touch it much less retrieve it. Elizabeth quickly tossed it into the water beside the other. She turned to the coven. "If this is our fate, then we must face it at once and turn the tide."

Free of the cave, Mary ran beside her mother and father, turning her head watching as the constable and his wife raced toward town. The magistrate's wife followed closely behind them. The Griggs' farm was now fully ablaze and the cowards wanted nothing to do with it. Ahead, horses reared and whinnied in the barn, panicked and trapped by the inferno. The house also burned; the thatch engulfed as hellish images danced upon the rooftop. Everything inside had already been lost, and anger seethed inside the woman as hotly as within the raging bonfires.

Elizabeth released her hold on Josiah. He blinked, suddenly aware of the state of his farm.

"How?" he demanded.

"Arson," Mary explained, then realized the culprit must be Curtis Charles.

The first thing Josiah did was hurry to the barn, throwing open the doors and freeing the horses. They raced past Elizabeth and Mary, charging into the night. The woman and girl stood alone among the tall stalks of sweet corn, horrified and dismayed.

"Remove your robe," Elizabeth commanded her daughter, pulling her own over her head. She shoved it into the girl's hands. "Hide these in the orchard," she said, "where none other than we shall find them."

Mary nodded and raced away.

The house had burned nearly to the ground by now, but the root cellar rested unscathed on the northern edge of the foundation. Elizabeth threw open the doors, the heat rushing past her as it escaped into the night. Heedless of the flames raging overhead, she disappeared into the dug-out basement. Rows of sweet potatoes, garlics, and onions rested in their cubbies, cooled by the soft dirt while bits of the floor tumbled down overhead.

Elizabeth knew the entire structure could topple soon, crushing her underneath and ending her life, but she would not tarry long. At the end of the row, beneath what had once been her bedroom, she pushed aside several wheels of cheese. These rolled in their waxy coverings, pushed by her fury. The panel here had been opened, revealing a hollow spot behind the shelves of pickled cabbage. Where there had once been two chests filled with her family's legacy, now there was disturbed dust with rectangular patches of emptiness.

The floorboards now creaked from the weight they bore, unable to hold up the house and ready to crash down one by one or as a unit. Elizabeth fled the cellar, racing into the night just as they let go behind her. The entire house toppled into the cavern beneath it, blazing upward with renewed fury.

Mary joined her side.

"It's gone," Elizabeth explained. "Stolen by the arsonist. The fire was to conceal their crime while tracks of their escape grew cold."

"We have to report it!" Mary suggested. "Tell Finneas Cooke at once!"

"Tell him *what*, exactly? That a fortune in Spanish gold and precious jewels were stolen from... from whom, *farmers*? It's one thing for him to practice mysticism, it's quite another to reveal our treasure! Besides, *he's gone,* along with the magistrate's wife! They fled from our side the moment they thought they would be revealed! Now it's gone! All of it at once! Whoever took it knew where to look. Rose Sadler must have known more than we thought."

"Who would she have told?" Mary asked.

"Who do you think? Who visited us just this very night?"

"Certainly not Curtis Charles!" Mary gasped.

Elizabeth looked up to find Josiah walking over. In his hands he carried a long black torch. She grabbed it, turning it over in her hands and examining it closely. "It's like those on the docks," she observed, then thrust it in front of her daughter. "We've seen this torch before, *haven't* we?" she demanded.

Mary's eyes grew wide with recognition. "Curtis Charles had it here in his hands when he visited. In his drunkenness he nearly lit the roof aflame."

"Well he succeeded in his task," Elizabeth declared. "Come, Daughter, we have work of our own while your father rounds up the animals." She led Mary toward the orchard, scooping up a chicken along the way.

No longer constrained by the rules of her grandmother's practice, Elizabeth Griggs worked another type of magic, darker and more sinister. The kind Molly Flannigan would not approve. It more closely resembled that which occurred earlier in the cave, involving a goat and a human heart. She drew out her knife and removed the head of the chicken, drawing a five pointed star on the ground.

"Mother!" Mary accused, shocked by the vile act of witchcraft.

But her mother ignored her protests and began chanting her curse. "Curtis Charles," Elizabeth said, dripping fresh blood over the image drawn in the dirt, placing upon it the torch that had destroyed her farm. It was a hex, one that would bind the boy for eternity. If he would defile them so, then the son of the ferryman would serve a different role.

"Dmnari porttitor animarum! Cupiditas divitiarum tibi serviat," Elizabeth said in Latin instead of Gaelic. "A slave you shall be, a slave to your lust for riches, damned to wander between worlds and a member of neither!"

She took the knife once more, wiping it clean on the sleeve of her dress then drawing it against the palm of her own hand. She let the warm stickiness drip, sealing the curse.

"Persolutionem, duos denarios pro quolibet victu!" she added. "Two coins is your fare, and payment must be exact!"

"What are you doing, Mother?" Mary demanded, aghast at the ritual. Tears filled her eyes, shocked by the ease with which her mother switched sides to darkness.

"Damned, you are, Curtis Charles," Elizabeth swore, "and may you be bound to honor as payment the first coins touched from this lot, so that I may face you once more and spit upon your face!" She drew two coins from the pouch around her neck and placed them beside the torch. Her daughter still held the blade pointed upward and Elizabeth gripped it tightly until her blood dripped onto Mary's fist. Then she squeezed it upon the blood payment, that which released the coins to Manann. She would offer them as her passage.

Exhausted, the woman and girl slumped on the ground, panting with eyes wide as the blood magic bound the items. The hex would work now, after Curtis Charles gave once more into his lust for treasure.

"Go now, Daughter," Elizabeth bade, "and draw your two coins from the water. You will need those when the Ferryman comes to call."

The girl nodded then fled, racing toward the lighthouse and cave below.

CHAPTER TEN

Dawn was breaking by the time Mary reached the cave. Making her way carefully down to the hidden passageway, she pondered the vision. *Mother hadn't even asked me about the rest of my vision. She only cared about the fire,* the girl realized. *I'm doomed to lunacy and she doesn't care!* Mary shuddered at the thought of ripping out her hair... her eyes.

But didn't she once say we can change our future? By the time Mary reached the pool, most of the torches had faded. Thankfully, they shimmered just enough to reveal two coins by the water's edge.

She waded in, pausing to stare at the hideous skulls smiling up at the doomed girl. *I lose my wits. I cut my own eyes out. Those gaping holes, how could I do this to myself? What kind of awfulness awaits me,* she wondered. She stooped to pick up the coins, pausing just before touching the gold. *Will I have another vision? Can I have another?* She paused so long the icy waters caused a shiver down her spine. Finally, she just scooped them up and ran, splashing, from the pool.

Collapsing on her knees, she found herself staring at the gutted goat, its empty eyes and out-hanging tongue watching her with judgement. *How can you be so pathetic,* it seemed to ask, *as to gouge your own eyes and rip out all your hair?*

"Shut up," she muttered to the animal, scrambling to her feet and running past the faded torches.

Before she reached the ramp, she froze in her tracks. Her eyes on the smiling skulls staring up from her palm. *These coins,* she

realized, *are as much of the problem as these witches I'm involved
with. Witches? My mother.* She yearned then, to race to the constable or magistrate and tell them all, that her parents were involved...
only... so were they, all of them involved.

Her next thought was of Curtis Charles. That sweet boy...
the sweet boy who burned down my home! Suddenly filled with
fury, she wanted Curtis Charles dead. No. *I want him damned!*

With trembling hands Mary raised the coins to her eyes,
pressing them against her lids as before. They did nothing. No
vision was revealed, not even a glimmer of the family playing in the
mansion at Castle Hill, or of the wretched woman in the asylum.
She choked back tears and kicked aside the lifeless goat still staring
at the pool.

She placed the useless coins into a pouch around her neck,
just as her mother carried hers.

A woman's voice from behind made Mary turn.

Ann Mason, the girl from the tavern inched her way down
the ramp into the cavern. "Where is it?" she demanded.

"Where's what?"

"The Ferryman's gold. We know it's here. I just can't figure
out where."

"Who is *we*? Did Rose Sadler tell you lies about my mother
and me?" Mary demanded.

"She told me about dealings in the dark and of witches and
mystics. I'm still trying to figure out which of those your mother
really is."

"Leave us alone, she's neither," Mary lied. Her mother was both.

"I know who burned your farm," Ann offered. "It was
William Mayes and a pirate, the dreaded Thomas Tew, not your
beloved Curtis Charles."

"Why are you telling me this?" Mary demanded.

"Because I come with an offer, an exchange that will return your family's wealth."

Mary stiffened. "What do you know of wealth?"

"I know Thomas Tew took yours, but he wants something else so badly he'll offer a trade."

"What kind of trade?" Mary asked, looking for a way out but also eyeing the woman carefully. She watched for any hint of swindle.

"This cave hides a secret, one that's worthless to you, but a true treasure to him. He wants the queen's coins, those marked with the image of the Ferryman himself."

"I don't know what you're talking about."

"Yes, you do. I was hidden there, just now behind those rocks when you came in. I saw you pick the coins from the water and place them to your eyes. Where are the rest? There's a chest full, somewhere, hidden either here or on your farm. Captain Tew will trade back both your chests of gold and jewels for that single box."

Mary froze in place, eyes darting to the rocks. Yes, someone could easily have hid there, and she would not have seen them when she came in. What really mattered was the chests, and how to get them back. "How do I know he'll keep his word?" she asked.

Ann shrugged. "Thomas Tew has plenty of treasure, he's the richest to sail either the Pirate's Round or Spanish Main. He spent years searching this island for that chest and would happily return what once belonged to your family in exchange."

Mary considered, the image of the family and that large mansion swimming briefly into her mind. *That could be* me, *instead of them, if I change my future with a single choice.* "There," she said, pointing toward the pool, "beyond the water."

Ann shook her head. "No. He looked there."

"I swear it is. Just last night, my father swam up from this pool and brought me mine." She held them up to the torchlight, the coins she wanted so badly to be rid of, as proof of something she could no longer offer in exchange.

Ann seemed thoughtful. "Another passageway then?"

"Maybe."

Without hesitating, the tavern maid ran into the water, diving down into its depths and swimming into the abyss.

Mary groaned, realizing she had to go too, and followed just as quickly. The water took her breath away, forcing her to pause and catch it once more before diving in. Downward she swam, searching the rocky bottom for an opening of any size. Twice she bumped into Ann Mason doing the same. After a while the girl beside her disappeared, her legs kicking forward. Mary moved where Ann had been and found a crevice, just big enough for a large man to swim through. Afraid she would never breathe air again, she kicked, pushing forward with her hands feeling along the passage walls.

Mary nearly reached the point of drowning halfway through, but sheer willpower drove her onward. Close to panic, she realized the journey had turned upward and kicked harder. Soon, a light appeared up ahead, daylight, it seemed, offering hope of air. Her lungs yearned for it, gulping against her tightly held lips and nearly forcing them to open. *I'll drown,* she realized, and kicked harder. The light grew larger ahead, giving a surge of strength to climb higher. At the last moment she gasped, just as sweet air surrounded her face. High above, daylight shone through a crack too small for a human to enter or leave. The only way out was the way she had entered.

I can't do that again!

Ann Mason had already arrived, treading water and searching the cavern. "Where is it?" she demanded.

"I don't know. I've never seen it." Looking around, Mary realized only a golden chalice remained of whatever coins were here.

"Say goodbye to the offer. Tew never barters twice," the tavern maid said, plunging beneath the surface and disappearing.

Mary looked around, fearing she would drown on the return trip, but also curious about the second chamber. It was tiny compared to the other, but easily assessable now that she knew the way in. A naturally occurring shelf revealed where a chest had recently sat. Though wet again with moisture, the perfectly smooth rectangle revealed where it had recently been. All of the coins were gone.

Mary thought of the rocks behind which Ann Mason had hid. She remembered the woman's words, that Thomas Tew and William Mayes had burned her home. *But no mention of Curtis Charles.* Her eyes grew wide with realization. He had lurked there, that night, and watched the ritual. After his friends created the distraction at the farm, he swam in and stole the chest, betraying the pirate and leaving the Griggs family to suffer their loss.

That's the way of it, she knew, the boy had betrayed everyone.

She plunged downward without another thought, swimming furiously to the other side. She would turn the tide of her fate, no matter what it did to Curtis Charles. She made the neck of the passage cleanly, much faster than before, and started to ascend. Upward, she climbed, determined to splash free and run straight to town. She would challenge Curtis Charles, demand he turn over the chest and...

Her hem caught ahold of sharp rocks, holding her in place as her held breath escaped. She would die here in this sunken passage.

Staring upward, Mary could see the pale glimmer of diminished torchlight, teasing her by lapping up the air with its flame. She could almost reach the surface, just beyond her outstretched hand. As she grasped, the torch above seeming to turn as if lighting the way for a vessel. It drew nearer until almost overhead.

The lack of oxygen clouded her vision and dark spots formed on the edges. Above, a face looked down, the eyes of the Ferryman replaced by golden coins. His face of three skulls laughed at her torment as he passed by, and she found another staring into the water. With eyes full of fear, Curtis Charles watched as Mary Griggs clutched at the surface. But she was no longer alone. Two more desperate souls pushed upward, unable like she to break the surface and scream for help. They shared in her agony as several more squeezed in around her, joined by hundreds and thousands of those gone mad.

On the boat above, Curtis fell backward. Off-balance he toppled, flailing arms as he slipped over the side. Desperation grabbed at the boy, pulling him under and Mary joined in with the other lost souls, eager to rip him asunder.

Hands gripped Mary, too, pulling her suddenly upward, toward the sweet air. She woke, coughing and sputtering the salty brine.

"You're welcome for saving you," Ann Mason muttered, "but all deals are off the table."

Mary watched the woman leave, feeling at the coins in the pouch around her neck, and pondered her future. *Cursed to eternal insanity, grasping for wits but never finding reason.* She touched her head, feeling the wet mass that now clumped and tangled like her thoughts. It itched her so, a terrible burden. Her nails dug deep as she scratched, absently digging out several strands by the roots, leaving lines of crimson along where there was once delicate skin.

CHAPTER ELEVEN

Elizabeth Griggs did not look up from her sweeping. The house was no more than embers and lumps of charcoal strewn all around her. "You took long enough," she told her daughter. "Did you get them?"

The girl said nothing, standing upon what was once the porch, dripping like a wet sack of uselessness.

"I said, did you get them?" Elizabeth took a closer look at her daughter, finding her in total disarray. Her dress was in tatters, with face puffy from tears and with lines of blood trailing down her scalp. "Great Jehovah!" the mother exclaimed, rushing to embrace her child. "What happened?"

The girl timidly lifted the pouch hanging from her neck. "I have them, but the others are gone." Her voice sounded eerie, as if she were someplace else, locked in a different reality than her surroundings.

"Which others?" Elizabeth demanded, grasping her daughter strongly by the shoulders. With a shake she asked again, "What do you mean, *others*?"

"All of the coins. The entire chest in the next chamber. Curtis Charles took them."

"How?" Elizabeth suddenly remembered the goat and the pentagram in the cave. "That thieving bastard!" Elizabeth cried out. "He's been seeking them, must have heard about them from Rose Sadler." Furious at the boy, she looked toward the torch and pair of coins laying on the pentagram. "We do this *now*," she decided, gathering a bundle of cloth in which to wrap the cursed items. Careful not to touch skin directly to any of the metal, she bundled them tightly and held them close to her chest.

The hex she had placed was not of her ancestors, it was something Rose Sadler had shown her. It was dark magic, practiced in the Caribbean and darker than any ritual she had ever dared. It was similar to a binding spell her own mother had taught but insisted should never be used in haste. These items were now instruments of hell, objects to damn Curtis Charles for eternity. He would become like Manann, his soul trapped forever between realms.

Resolute in exacting her revenge, she grasped her daughter by the wrist.

"I don't want to!" Mary screamed stubbornly, pulling away. "I'm tired of this, I've seen so much, already! I'm going to die a spinster! I'm already losing my mind, Mother!" To prove her point, she grabbed fistfuls of her hair and yanked them free, holding bloody roots up for inspection. Her eyes, wild as one who has completely lost their wits, dared Elizabeth to argue.

A simple slap across the face was all it took, and the girl stared stunned as if it were the first time. It wasn't of course, not regarding *this* petulant child, whose insolence bordered on free thought.

"We go *now*!" Elizabeth commanded and shoved the child into the yard.

Josiah had already hitched the wagon, the horses finally recovered from the night's ordeal. He sat atop the bench, waiting, knowing his wife had business in town. Elizabeth carried the bundle, never setting it down even briefly, and waited for Mary to climb into the back.

"Drive," she commanded her husband.

Twenty solemn minutes later, they arrived outside White Horse Tavern, stepping down to proceed on foot.

"Where does he live?" Elizabeth asked her daughter.

"Up the way, down Touro street to Clarke. Near the Clarkeston Inn," Mary said with vacant eyes.

Elizabeth almost felt compassion then for her daughter, but it was *her* fault this young man had come so close to their family secrets. She had brought the devil to their doorstep, allowing him to sniff around their home and steal away their wealth. It was time to confront him, to seal his fate with the items in the bundle.

By the time they found the house, the morning had mostly gone. The crowd moved up and down the street making good cover. No one seemed to notice the simple family of farmers watching the building.

"I can go in," Josiah offered, "and search his room."

"We *all* will," Elizabeth decided, watching her daughter closely. The girl had changed so much since her vision, weak, and trapped by fear.

"I don't want to," Mary whimpered.

"You *will*. It's time you learn the truth about this witch who moved against our family."

"But my vision! It was so real, I..."

"The madness you saw isn't for certain," Elizabeth insisted. "You *can* change your fate."

Mary nodded, but her vacant eyes only stared.

They crossed the street, finding the door to his small craftsman home unlocked but firmly shut. Elizabeth took a deep breath then turned the knob, pushing it open and stepping inside.

The sight inside was gruesome. A girl, that tavern maid Ann Mason, lay stripped naked and spread across the five points of the pentagram. Her lifeless eyes stared upward. Elizabeth turned quickly, clamping her hand over Mary's mouth as it opened to scream.

"Don't do that! You'll bring the town, and they'll believe *we* did this!"

Mary nodded, her eyes no longer vacant but instead wide with fear.

Elizabeth removed her hand, then pointed at Curtis Charles on the bed, adding, "Or worse, you'll wake *him*!" He was fully dressed but with clothing torn and tattered. Blood had dried on his face, smeared about his mouth. Motionless and barely breathing, he was locked in a vision, staring upward with eyes covered by two golden coins, each with the Ferryman's mark.

Mary walked to the bed and stared down at him. "Why did he do that to her, Mother?"

"This woman's heart is gone. Look at the blood on his mouth, I'm certain he ate it," Elizabeth proclaimed.

Mary recoiled. "Why? Why would Curtis Charles do such a thing?"

"For immortality or to muster strength for walking in the spirit realm. He's no doubt there now, neither dead nor alive, and not planted in either realm."

"He's really a witch?" Mary asked, still refusing to believe. She tugged at her hair and scratched furiously her scalp.

"Yes, and now I'm certain he's the one who sacrificed the goat in our cave. He was searching for every trace of our treasure, drawn by greed for wealth but also the power of the Ferryman's coins. See here how he uses them now? Locked in his vision and unaware we're even here."

"No," Mary abruptly spoke, turning the heads of both her parents. "Ann Mason offered me a deal, claiming Captain Tew has our treasure and would trade it for the Ferryman's coins. Curtis Charles never even knew about it! I don't know how he found out about the coins, but he never knew about our treasure."

Elizabeth paused, shocked by the new information. "Thomas Tew has our fortune?"

"Yes. *He* burned our home and stole our chests, not Curtis Charles. This boy only watched our ritual and waited till we left. Then he swam in and stole the Ferryman's coins, meaning to keep them for himself."

Elizabeth shot a look to her husband. "Find the coins, they may still be here!"

"Mother?" Mary asked, watching as her father wildly tossed the room, searching for the chest.

"It's a good deal he offered. I'd gladly trade those wretched items for our wealth."

Josiah threw open the closet, kneeling to search every corner. Finding nothing, he turned to his wife, shaking his head. "They must have been here but now are gone."

"Perhaps Thomas Tew already took them," Mary suggested, "and Curtis isn't guilty at all! Maybe he's a victim, like us!"

Elizabeth balked at the suggestion. "Your beloved Curtis Charles wasn't doubled crossed. Look here!" She pointed at the sacrificed woman. "He's a witch, child! He deserves the fate we gave him!"

"We?" Mary turned, her eyes no longer vacant nor terrified. They screamed with anger. "*You* cursed him with that fate! *You* drew the devil's attention with that spell! What I saw you do to his torch wasn't white magic, and you can't call it mysticism!"

Elizabeth froze, her hands wrapped around the swaddled bundle. She slowly peeled back layer after layer until the torch was exposed. The time had come, it was time to damn the young man. "Go after Thomas Tew," she told her husband. "Find him and let's retrieve what's ours."

"He'll be headed to his ship," Josiah offered, hurrying from the tiny apartment.

Careful not to touch the metal, Elizabeth pressed it into Curtis's hand, muttering the same words she had used before, "Dmnari porttitor animarum! Cupiditas divitiarum tibi serviat." The hex complete, he would forever be a slave to his fate. "Persolutionem, duos denarios pro quolibet victu!"

After she had finished, she leaned the torch against the corner where he would surely find it upon awakening. The two coins came next, shaken free of the bundle and falling beside its base.

"You've *cursed* him, Mother! You're a witch. No better than he!" Mary accused.

"Maybe so, child, but this man deserved it." Her business here concluded, she opened the door and stepped out onto the street, leaving her daughter to find her own way.

Mary watched her mother depart, staring at the door as it slammed, shutting her inside with the corpses. She stared at the man she had been ready to love. He, like her mother, was a witch, and she found him repulsive. He was a drunkard, a thief, as well. His lips, once rosy and kissable, were now grey and lifeless. How could she have loved him, this despicable excuse for a man?

She wondered at his final hex, the killing of an innocent woman. *Was it as Mother said? Did he kill her to achieve eternal life?* Mother had also said he ate this poor woman's heart, and the dried blood on his lips agreed.

But, inside her gut, she wondered if any of what her mother accused was true. With trembling hand, the girl lifted his wrists and turned them over, inspecting his palms for evidence supporting that claim. They, like the torch in the corner, were clean without even a trace of blood.

She peered, searching for the source of the blood and placed her hand beside his arm to lean closer.

He abruptly grabbed her arm and waist, pulling her against his body with ear close to his mouth. The room seemed to spin as he whispered, "Join me in fate, Mary Griggs. Join me..."

Locked tightly in his arms, all she could see was the torch in the corner. The rest of her vision blurred by tears.

In her mind, Mary joined with him, taken on a journey into another realm. She was suddenly in the White Horse, watching as Curtis Charles ate his meal. Ann Mason was there as well, cleaning up and ready to close for the night. Other than them, the place was empty.

Something felt odd in this place, the air was neither cold nor hot, having no feeling at all. There was no smell in this vision, not even from the stew in his bowl.

"Your girlfriend and I spoke today. She asked about Rose Sadler and demanded to know what she told me about them," Ann said.

"She was right about them. They're witches, both of them," he replied, sniffing the stew and frowning.

"They made that known to me as well, threatening curses and the like. But I didn't speak, gave nothing up at all. Not even that Tew would never give up their precious gold, not even for those odd coins. That thought's amusing, isn't it? Knowing they hid away that wealth and will never enjoy it? Let them look and wonder where it went, I say. It's lost to them till judgement day damns them to hell and their dark lord tells them!" She let out a chuckle. "Serves them both right, the evil bitches."

He put a spoonful of stew into his mouth, chewing it slowly then shoving it aside. Then he swallowed a mug of ale and frowned again.

"You should go now," Ann suggested, "I want to close up and get some rest."

Curtis rose and moved toward the door, pausing as he turned to ask one more question. "This *Tew* cents. Was it the same he paid me? Two of those strange coins?"

She nodded, scooping up his uneaten dinner and full mug of ale. "Aye, worthless ones at that."

"I'd keep them on you. They may come in handy later," he said, then stepped outside into the night.

Mary followed him outside, walking alongside as he made his way to the docks.

"You shouldn't be here," he snapped, suddenly aware of her presence.

Abruptly, she found herself standing on a beach. The night was the same, lacking smell or feeling, but she wasn't alone. There were people here, awful ones at that. Each of them seemed desperate, lost and ambling around as if searching for something.

No, she thought, *not searching. Waiting!*

Waiting, but for what or whom?

"Who is it?" she demanded, stopping a woman from her meanders. Dressed in puritan attire, the lady stared back with vacant eyes. "Who are we waiting for?"

"Must make it to the other side," the lady muttered.

"Other side? Other side of what? To where? I don't understand."

The lady's eyes came into focus, as if seeing Mary for the first time. She recoiled with disgust and proclaimed, "I'm waiting to go to heaven, a place in which you'll never step foot!"

Mary turned to peer across the water, certain now a place waited on the other side. Off in the distance she made out a boat. Others saw it as well, rushing to water's edge and waving their arms frantically to be seen.

The puritan lady reached the water, touching the hem of her dress against its waves. She screamed, pulling back from searing heat. The cloth, instead of being wet, burned as if it had touched fire instead. Others met the same torment, pushing desperately close to the edge and crying out with anguish. Behind Mary others surged, pushing the mob. Someone shoved her forward, sending her dangerously close to the burning waters. Another push sent her falling, with arms flailing against the pending splash.

Her eyes shot open, finding herself laying on the floor beside Curtis Charles' bed.

"Get up!" Elizabeth Griggs shouted, grabbing her daughter and hauling her onto unsteady legs.

Mary turned as her mother dragged her out, staring at her suitor still staring upward through those cursed coins. His eyes... those coins... to her they were now one and the same.

CHAPTER TWELVE

Elizabeth and Josiah sat inside the constable's office, deep in conversation with Finneas Cooke. He had sent away his deputies, and the trio spoke freely without fear of being overheard. Mary, though hearing their words, stared out the window with disinterest. More interesting to her than their accusations and conspiracies were the screams and wails on the beach. Part of her remained there, burning and drowning in that pool of madness. She alternated between realities now, here staring out the window and there burning in anguish.

"We want him arrested tonight, Finneas!" Elizabeth demanded.

"Arrested, but no trial! He'll say things that will damn us all," the constable argued. "If he was in that cave then he saw me, too!" He rubbed his head where the blow had struck him, knocking him unconscious. No, he wanted the boy *dead*.

"The torch is there, evidence of his arson, and so is the body of Ann Mason. He killed her in a dark ritual, the same as you found in the cave!" Elizabeth pleaded.

Finneas shuddered at the memory. He and Sally had arrived early, unaware someone lurked there already. They came across the dark ritual, the sacrificed goat, and the pentagram, and were pondering its meaning when the blow came down hard against his temple. Sally, too concerned with her husband's well-being and much too frightened to interfere with his assailant, had cowered down and seen nothing recognizable. Josiah, in his vacant state, was no help either, having walked past the pair and entered the water without seeing them or the goat.

By the time Mary and Elizabeth arrived, Sally was already chanting over her husband and had no choice but to assist the mystic healing. Mary shivered at that memory, her second delve into mysticism in a few short hours. She would never be the same after that night, not by what she had aided them in or what she, herself, would experience later. Thinking of it now forced her to relive the horrors, granting brief respite from the pain of the water's edge. But too quickly her mind returned there, again going through the torment.

"What if he never makes it to trial?" Josiah asked. "Let *me* have a crack at him. Me and the townsfolk! He'll try and accuse my wife and daughter, and so we must prove he is the witch, not they. Let him make the pronouncement, then lock him here and send your deputies away. I'll come around midnight, and we'll do it the old way. He'll swing from the tallest tree!"

"As constable I can't condone lynching," Finneas frowned, but that was exactly what he wanted, himself.

"Go somewhere else, then," Elizabeth suggested. "Be seen in another part of town, and you'll be clear of misconduct."

"I don't know, none of this brings back the coins. Thomas Tew left port hours ago, and we've no way to get them back."

"Damn them, and damn *him*! We've lost everything, and all I can have is my revenge!" Elizabeth demanded.

"That's not enough to turn my eye, and you know it. Pay me something, at least!"

"Pay you?" Elizabeth leaned across his desk. "How about I tell the town that we *are* witches, and that you and Sally lead the coven? They'd spare us for turning over the true threat to Newport!"

"You *wouldn't*!"

"No? Then you've no idea how much I *need* this revenge!"

"Okay! Fine! I'll do it. Just make sure you wait till midnight so I can leave on the ferry. I'll take Sally to Providence and be seen there."

Mary heard her parents and the constable exchange more, but she was now thoroughly lost in the other realm. Others had fallen into the water, burning and drowning alongside her. The lines on her head, those where she had scratched away her hair, throbbed with heat as well. She reached up and picked at a spot, scabbed and trying to heal, the only way she had found to bring relief.

She felt Elizabeth drag her away from the office.

"Let's go," her mother said gruffly. "We need baths and to rest up for this evening." Shoving her out the door. They made their way back to Clarke Street, Elizabeth desiring to overlook Curtis Charles' apartment. She wanted to watch and to follow him once he awakened, curious to see how he tried to hide Ann Mason's body.

Mary had mostly regained her senses, feeling more in her own realm than the other, and followed her mother and father as they walked. Most of the people they passed were pleasing to look upon, warmly inviting and less horrific than those in her vision. Finding comfort, she gazed into each of their eyes, counting how many blue, or green, or brown she encountered. Most smiled back, happy to see a pretty face, then frowned at the blood in her hair.

But then one face in particular caused her to pause. Dressed all in black, the woman's dress reached the ground, hiding her ankles. On her shoulders was a white shawl, hanging low to ensure no bit of her blouse opened up. Upon her head she wore a tight bonnet, one that hid her hair in case it should incite a man's lust. Her eyes, unlike the others were hollow pits without orbs.

Mary did not scream. She had already seen so many horrifying things in the past two days. She merely gasped and looked away from the puritan's stare. Doing so landed her gaze on a man, dressed in a sixteenth century sailing frock, staring back with another set of gouged out holes. Mary lowered her eyes to the ground and hurried to catch up to her parents.

Thankfully, they quickly arrived and found rooms in the Clarkeston Inn. They took two, one for Mary and another because her parents wanted privacy. The pair were still hatching plots against Curtis Charles, but also planning a way to find and take on Thomas Tew. Elizabeth, especially, had grown obsessed with finding her family's treasure.

A bath was soon drawn, and Mary took her turn last, while the water was only lukewarm. No matter the temperature she found no respite, finding it as scalding as that within her vision.

A voice from the corner of the room spoke softly, preaching fire and brimstone. "Filthy child," the lady in the black dress accused, "scrub both your body and soul!"

Mary struggled then, to come clean, feeling dirtier with each pass of the washcloth. She pressed harder, until her nails found skin and scraped away the offensive skin. All of it had to go, she realized, all that had touched that filthy water.

"You've touched the evil arts," the puritan lady said from a chair in the corner, "and you're doomed to wander the shoreline till he comes."

Mary scrubbed harder as she listened, intent on her task, and never noticing her mother had entered the room.

Elizabeth pushed open Mary's door, meaning to chat a bit before resting up for the busy night ahead. The past two days had been hard on all of them, but especially the girl. It was time to discuss her vision, to console any worries and come up with a plan to ensure it would never come true. She, herself, had seen bad ones so terrifying they would have driven a weaker person mad. But there's always a way to avoid what you see, or at least that's what her own mother ensured.

"It's time we have a talk," she said as she entered the room, but froze in place as soon as she did. The warm towels, meant to dry the girl, tumbled from her arms and onto the floor.

Mary sat in the tub, oblivious to her mother's arrival, streaked with red and sitting in crimson water. Blood oozed everywhere, dripping down her face, her arms, her chest. Tufts of hair, ripped free of her scalp, floated on the surface or lay discarded on the floor. Her mutterings revealed a tenuous grip on sanity.

"He's coming for me, seeking for me now. The Ferryman comes!"

"Mary," Elizabeth pleaded softly, kneeling beside the tub and gently pulling the child's hands from her scalp. "Listen to me, Mary. Whatever you saw, it isn't certain! You can change it. *We* can change it!"

But any sanity the girl once held had slipped through her grasp. Lifting her head to meet her mother's eyes, she uttered the following,

"Atropos, Clotho, and I am the big brother.
Listen to my Servant, and you might not suffer.
Tread carefully around the ferry,
As he holds your obituary,
Though I seem to wind and wander,
There are lessons in the water.
His duty is to ferry you,
Oarless and without an answer to the end."

Elizabeth had heard these words before, but could not believe the source of them now. "What is that you speak, child? Where did you hear it, Mary?"

The girl lifted a scarlet finger outward, pointing to an empty rocker in the corner of the room.

"What is it? What do you see?"

"Don't you see the woman?"

"No, Mary." Elizabeth stared at the empty chair, watching and worried. She would have to call the doctor now to deal with this madness. But then the rocker began to move lightly back and forth, growing stronger with each movement. Elizabeth gasped, suddenly very afraid, and realizing her daughter's sanity remained intact. "Who is she? Who are you speaking to, Mary?"

"I met her on the seashore, Mother. Her name is Molly Flannigan, and she says what you've done amounts to blasphemy. Blasphemy against God and unholy beneath his judgment."

Elizabeth shivered against the sudden cold in the room. "My grandmother is *here*?" Though she could not see the specter, she imagined the woman rocking, dressed in puritanical black and condemning her descendants for witchcraft.

"She also says the Ferryman is coming, coming for us all. And we must know the answer to his riddle when he does."

Elizabeth stood, horrified by her daughter's words, and ran from the room. They needed fire to deal with Curtis Charles, a simple hanging would not do.

CHAPTER THIRTEEN

Elizabeth Griggs watched the clock above the mantle. It neared midnight. Soon, her husband would enter the jail and remove the boy. A quick glance out the window confirmed torches near the square, meaning they were on their way. She looked then at her daughter, a wretched sight even while napping peacefully, and prayed the curse would be lifted.

That's what she had decided it was, a curse placed by Curtis Charles when he stole the Ferryman's gold. He was the only person who could have performed the ritual in the cave, and most certainly the man who knocked out Finneas Cooke. *Mary's feet*, she had realized, were standing atop the pentagram when she divined her fate with the coins.

Why had I not realized this before? She thought then of the riddle the girl recited in the bath. The answer to it was *fate*, of course, and she had been cursed with an altered version of hers. The only way to lift the curse was to commit the person who set it to fire. The flames would cleanse Curtis Charles, removing the power he held over Mary.

She knelt by her daughter's side and gently shook her awake. "Rise," she said. "It's time."

Mary yawned and stretched, her eyes once again locked on the rocker in the corner. "She hasn't left, Mother. She says we are fools, that we must burn ourselves for the curses we placed."

"She's ignorant to the circumstances, Daughter, and dead and buried as well. She has no bearing over our lives. As soon as Curtis Charles burns, you will never see her again."

"I hope you're right."

Elizabeth watched as Mary absently scratched at her scalp, opening up a freshly scabbed wound. "Stop that," she barked, and watched the girl's hand fall to her side.

"My skin burns so badly, Mother. My eyes, too. I can't stand these orbs in my head."

"That, too, will stop," Elizabeth promised, "after he is burned."

The pair dressed themselves, pulling shawls over their shoulders before venturing into the night. As they stepped out, they saw the torches had reached the jail. The clock above the courthouse rang out twelve bells, signaling midnight and Curtis Charles' fateful release. They hurried then toward the square, finding shadows to hide in just outside the blacksmith's shop.

Josiah and the mob soon rounded Marlborough Street, leading Curtis Charles by a chain connected to his shackles. To Elizabeth's disgust, the boy held his head high, full of pride and arrogance to the end.

Soon, they reached the pyre and Josiah ran the chain through a ring several inches above the boy's head, then wrapped it several times around his body before locking it in place. This was done for two reasons. First as a display of his guilt to those gathered, but also to bind the witch by iron until the hex was lifted. To aid in this process, hidden by all gathered, Josiah had painted a five pointed star beneath Curtis Charles' feet. His death would be the ultimate sacrifice, unraveling his own rituals, and freeing Mary of her damnation.

In the boy's pocket, Josiah would have placed two coins. These were Mary's, and those in his purse were her own. She had pledged him to the realm between realms, unable to pay his own passage, but forced to honor theirs. Her hope was to seal his fate, keeping him far away from her family.

Josiah lit the torch, the same Curtis had used to burn their home, lighting the base and stepping back, tossing the cursed instrument at the boy's feet. This, too, would complete the hex, helping to anchor him in that empty place.

From beside Elizabeth, Mary picked up a stool and strode forward.

"Come back here!" the mother whispered, but the girl did not obey.

Placing the stool in front of the flaming pyre, still low and not yet an inferno, she stepped up and peered into the boy's eyes.

Mary stepped onto the stool, letting the sound of crackling flame drown out the whispers of Molly Flannigan. Curtis Charles' eyes blinked open as she reached his height, staring back at her with anger and malice. The crowd chanted as he burned, damning him to hell and decrying all others like him.

"Die, witch, die!" they said in unison, but his defiance told Mary he wanted to *kill* instead of die.

Mary reached a hand into his pocket, saying, "These are your payment, Curtis Charles," Mary whispered into his ear. "You'll become something different now, and I give them to you freely. In return, I want a different future than I saw."

"I would have loved you," he managed through clenched teeth, the pain unlike any he'd ever felt.

"It would have been unrequited," she assured him, placing the coins to his eyes and pressing firmly with her thumbs. She yearned to push them deeper. "Look," she whispered, "into the future and find your fate."

He laughed, a devilish sound from a dying witch. "Oh, Mary," he said loud enough the mob hushed. "Don't you see what you've done? You and Elizabeth are cursed by your own mistake! A *grave* one, certain to haunt you forever. I see my fate, sure, but it far out reaches your own!"

"Shut up," the girl hissed, pressing the coins harder into his eyes.

"That's just it! I can't stop! I've seen my fate, lived it already, and there's *nothing* left for me to fear! These coins you show me, I've already seen," he said. "Yours are in my pocket, and these I left for you to find! You show my own fate I have already seen!"

"Step back, Mary!" Josiah commanded. "His curses will damn you, even if the flames only catch your hem!"

But Mary would not heed. She leaned in closer, full of rage and fury, hellbent on changing the course of her own destiny.

"Take back what I saw!" she demanded. "Change my fate, at least the part regarding *you*!" The fact Curtis did not cry out forced her fingers and the coins deeper into his skull, tokens now of deeper meaning than what her mother once intended.

"I need only two," Curtis said calmly, just as the jelly within his orbs ruptured. "The curse demanded you pay me passage, two coins to carry you upon your way, but you paid the wrong amount."

"Right amount," Mary insisted, driving the gold deep into his skull. "Two coins for the Ferryman!"

"Only you haven't paid me two," Curtis explained. "You paid me three while your mother paid me one!"

"You are a liar and a drunk! I *hate* you, Curtis Charles! I will *not* live the fate I saw!"

"You will," the dying man whispered, because you paid me before your journey even began.   These coins you show me, I've already seen," he said. "Yours are in my pocket, and these I left for you to find! You show my own fate I have already seen!"

Mary lost her footing, falling backward, landing hard with a crack. Breathless, she stared upward into the coins that were once his eyes. He never shouted out as the flames, now raging high and full, licked at his flesh. The inferno raged, backlighting a horrifying transformation. The skin melted off Curtis Charles, dripping like tallow and sparking the fire higher. It yearned for his tinder, hungered for his flesh, and consumed every bit of softness, leaving only his bones and two coins behind. These smiled, laughing and damning her soul with a curse of their own.

Mary screamed, unable to hide her terror—not at the image burning before her, but for their mistake. If he was right, then she and her mother had brought damnation upon themselves. There was no way now to recover either these coins or the pair left behind with the torch.

Curtis Charles had died. In his place only the Ferryman remained.

Elizabeth knelt down beside her daughter, cradling her in motherly arms. "It's finished, now, Daughter."

"My coins," Mary asked with a trembling voice. "Only I touched them, right?"

Elizabeth paused, remembering that night in the cave. "Yes, I..." but that was a lie. One had dropped in the water, while another landed on the rocks. *I picked that one up, and tossed it into the water.* "Of course!" she lied again.

"The coins I found at the water's edge were not my own, Mother. They always gave me a different fate. He says he took them, claiming my fare and leaving two more for me to find. Two, he claims, showing me his fate instead of my own."

Elizabeth felt her stomach lurch. Not only had she touched the coin, marking it as payment from her, the sum would include the two she had placed in his pocket. She had paid three, while Mary paid only one.

We're doomed, she thought, looking up at the image of her grandmother now standing before her.

"Doomed to Hell as witches," Molly Flannigan agreed, "and the Ferryman will take you there soon!"

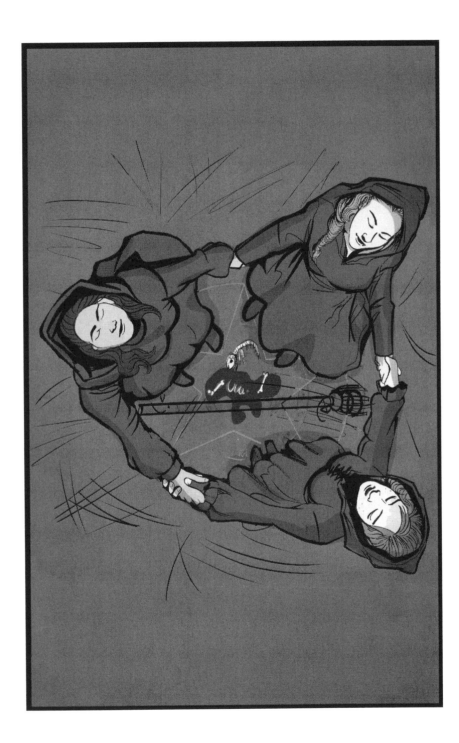

PART III
THE PIRATE

CHAPTER FOURTEEN

Castle Hills, Rhode Island Colony, Two Days Earlier

Thomas Tew, Captain of *Amity*, a seventy-ton sloop, was a privateer sanctioned by the Governor of Bermuda. Recently, he had turned to piracy by freer offerings of success. A resident of Newport, Rhode Island, this former nobleman sat dejected and damp in a cave beneath the rocks of Castle Hills, Rhode Island. He had been hiding out here for days, searching for something so dark, so disgusting, it rivaled his own existence. He *had* to find it, if only to expand his own wealth and those from whom he may bribe when seeking pardons. But, right now, he was tired of the cave.

So far, all he found was rock walls and a chilling pool of water at its termination.

He needed air and made his way topside for a sweeter breath. He sat there, with the door open, gulping in the freshness. It was a strange door, one made many years ago to cloak the entrance, with faux rock affixed to a wooden portal. Had he not been so persistent in his searching, he never would have found it. Thankfully, he stumbled upon it by chance, slipping while drunk and crashing his shoulder into a resounding *clunk* that proved the stone fake. It had swung open on its own and given him instant hope he would find the Ferryman's gold.

Only false hope, so far.

Thankful for air, he yearned to shout obscenities at the sun, so vulgar while shining into his eyes, but showed discernment when two women suddenly stepped down the embankment.

The girl, peering out over the bay, chided her mother. "I see water, Mother. Water and rocks, not wealth."

Tew perked up at mention of wealth.

"More wealth has crashed upon these rocks over the years than has grown in the tilled fields we own. There was a reason Grandfather Flannigan built this beacon, and it was to hide his riches in plain sight," the mother said.

Thomas Tew strained his ears to listen.

"I don't understand," the girl admitted.

"Ever since Europeans found the Americas, they've been plundering its riches and crashing them against rocks like these. That's what Grandfather Flannigan found when he settled here in 1636. He was fed up with Roger Williams, a rebellious young firebrand chased out of every other Puritan congregation."

"He split away from Providence? I thought he settled here directly," the girl pondered.

"He originally sailed with Williams but secretly ventured out to find a plot of land to call his own. He found these rocks, on this shore, and a treasure hidden beneath centuries of debris. He gathered it all, piece of eight by piece of eight, until he amassed a fortune of gold and jewels."

Thomas grinned at that. *A fortune, here?* This was a bonus, something he had not expected. They were departing, so he scrambled up the hill to follow. Keeping a distance so as not to be seen, he watched as they reached the Griggs' farm. *So this is Elizabeth Griggs,* he thought with a smile. The woman and her husband were known to him, though he had never laid eyes on either.

Elizabeth led her daughter into a root cellar beneath the house, leaving the door open for light. The captain considered whether he should creep closer, but spied her husband by the barn. It wouldn't do to spark a fight with the man, a behemoth with a legendary temper. Thomas would have to wait until nightfall, then return with his crew.

White Horse Tavern was busy when he arrived, and Thomas Tew hid easily among the fishermen. Dressed simply, he wore a hooded cloak that concealed his face as well as his weapons. The short sword was more of a knife, broad and long, but strapped neatly to his upper leg. Should he have need to draw it, though, he would not fight alone. Cole McLain was there, his first mate aboard *Amity*.

"Did you find it?" McLain asked.

"She was right about the cave. I found it just where she said, well disguised along the seawall."

"And the gold? Was it there?"

"If it is, I can't find its hiding place. I saw nothing but rocks and a pool of water."

"Did you look inside the pool?"

"I dove in and swam around a bit, but it was too dark to see anything. Feeling around only discovered more rocks. I'm going back tonight as soon as I've eaten. There's something else, though, an opportunity we can't pass up."

McLain's interest was perked. "What is it, Captain? What'cha got?"

"It seems the Griggs family likes to pick up more than seashells from the beach. They've got more than a hundred years of sea bounty hidden away in their root cellar. Are you up to that job while I try the cave again?"

"Of course I am."

"Good. Take along a few of the boys. Josiah Griggs is a bear of a man and will defend his home. I need food." Thomas Tew locked eyes with Ann Mason across the room, signaling her to approach. She was a pretty gal, buxom and pleasingly capable of intelligent conversation. With his family left behind in Bermuda, this girl provided a decent distraction when the need aroused.

Catching his signal, she nodded, and casually walked over as if he were a normal customer. "Good evening, gents," she said with her usual smile. "What can I get you?"

"Some of that stew would be good," Thomas said, waving her closer to whisper before adding, "and bit of help tonight with an... opportunity."

"What kind of opportunity?" she asked, masking her excitement.

"Who around here knows the Griggs' farm well enough and would be looking for a job as crewman?"

"Curtis Charles knows the family, he's smitten by their daughter, but he'd make a piss poor crewman. Afraid of the water, that one! But he hangs around William Mayes. Of the two, Mayes is your best bet," she offered.

Thomas laughed. "The tavern owner? He's too old and set in his ways."

"I meant his son. He's wide-eyed and yearning for adventure. Bugs me every time he's in here about what pirates I know. He sailed with William Kidd for a bit, though, so his interest's legitimate in piracy."

"That's such a crass term," the captain said with a frown. "I prefer *businessmen* and *entrepreneurial reinvestment*." He and McLain shared a laugh.

"He'd be eager to hire on, hates it here in Newport. What's the job? What should I tell him?"

"I need him to help make a distraction at the farm tonight. McLain here needs to get into their root cellar. Turns out that family's sitting on a treasure of wealth."

Ann laughed. "Surely not the Griggs family! They're poor farmers. Rose Sadler told me that, herself! Said they've got nothing to their name, just those weird coins down in the cave."

"Turns out they've got wealth, for sure, and we're taking it tonight. Now go fetch my dinner."

"Fine," she said, musing as she walked away.

Tew watched Ann go about her job, tending to customers and fetching his dinner. "I've another way to find the coins," he told McLain. "I used it once, down in the Caribbean. One of those voodoo witches taught it to me, a way to divine any object that's been hexed, even after that hex is lifted."

McLain's eyes grew big. Every man in Tew's service knew about his penchant for the dark arts. That was one of his draws, back when he announced the vote to switch to piracy. He was lucky, brought them all the biggest haul ever by a pirate crew, all without even firing a shot. The first mate nodded. "A gold chain or wooden leg, I'll stand with you, Captain!"

"Good. Now go find me a goat while I finish my dinner."

Later that evening, Ann Mason watched Curtis Charles closely, pleased at the ire she had gently pushed into his temper.

"Are you suggesting," Curtis asked her flatly, "my Mary may be a witch?"

"Stranger things have proved true," the barmaid said with a shrug. "Margaret Murphy was accused and burned for her sins. Perhaps your Mary's guilty as well."

"I've heard enough," Curtis decided, standing to leave. He staggered drunkenly from the ale, clearly unable to handle his night's consumption.

"Rose Sadler," Ann said flatly, causing both young men to pause. "I heard it from Rose Sadler that both Mary and her mother, Elizabeth, are witches."

"Rose Sadler was executed for witchcraft six months ago," Curtis said over his shoulder. "When did she tell you this?"

"Just before. She claimed to be of their coven, but they gave *her* up as a scapegoat so they would live. Rose told me that, if any accusations were made about her, to know it was the Griggs."

"I won't believe it," Curtis said.

"Did she leave proof?" William demanded.

"She knew the whereabouts of Le Sage's treasure. Claimed it was on the Griggs' farm, hidden in a cave beneath the lighthouse."

"Nonsense," Curtis exclaimed, making his way to the door.

As soon as the heavy wood slammed behind him, Ann grabbed William Mayes' shoulder. "Do you really want to meet Captain Tew?"

"Seriously?" The boy nearly came out of his chair.

"Sure enough! All you have to do is get that drunken sot up to see his girl tonight. Make a distraction, any kind, that gets them out of the house. Hell, set their barn on fire if you can."

"Why? What's in it for me?" he asked with suspicion.

"Remember Rose Sadler's story? About the gold hidden under the lighthouse?"

"Yeah? So?"

"Turns out it's under the house in their root cellar. Tew's taking it tonight. If you help, you can even join his crew."

"You can't be serious. You're pulling my leg!"

"Not at all, now go catch your friend. Get him up to the Griggs' farm without delay."

It was so easy, working these boys into a frenzy, and Ann Mason laughed as William dashed from the tavern.

CHAPTER FIFTEEN

Thomas Tew found himself once more in that damp, uninteresting cave. The only sound, besides the screaming in his thoughts, was the slow and infuriating dripping of water into a pool. That pool, the bane of his problem, hid answers he was running out of time to unravel. He would have to shove off soon, making the round. To be successful, he would have to reach Cape Town, and get around Cape Agulhas, before summer. Otherwise, he would have to wait another year to raid the Moghuls of the Indian subcontinent.

The sudden bleat of a goat snapped Thomas from his thoughts, and he responded by kicking the animal hard in the ribs. It cried and pulled away on its rope. Such a pathetic creature, weak and lacking courage. *Death will be its mercy*, he thought.

A bundle lay nearby, full of torches brought to light the pool. He placed these around the water's edge, leaning them over the glasslike surface. He lit them quickly, eager for their illumination, then peered into the depths. More rocks were all he found.

He drew his knife, long and broad, and furiously dug into the sandy floor. First he drew a five pointed star, the pentagram, symbolic of humanity over gods. Each point, connected by continuous lines, represented the human form. The head, outstretched arms and legs, and the central torso containing vital organs, fit perfectly into this image. Power resided within the center, power that proved mankind were equal to or superior to their gods.

Thomas loved this symbol. It reminded him of himself—superior to all others. He learned its true meaning in the Caribbean where voodoo witches raised the dead and punished their enemies from afar. He spent many years learning their ways, preparing for the day he could once more uncover Dee's coins—those meant for Queen Elizabeth and her loyalists. The ignorant called them the Ferryman's coins, claiming they would serve as passage to the afterlife. There was no Ferryman, Thomas knew, because there was no afterlife and mankind were the only gods.

He completed his drawing with a large circle, carefully touching and not disrupting each tip of the star. The head pointed toward the pool, necessary for what would come next. This ritual of sight required blood, and for that he turned toward the goat. Its up-staring eyes seemed to understand, and it pulled and bleated at the rope, gnawing for its life.

Tew grabbed the animal by two hooves, flipping it hard onto its side. With braided line he lashed its legs to prevent escape, then carried it over to the pentagram. Dangled over the center, it wriggled and complained, unaware of the mercy slice to come. The blade drew clean, spilling blood into the center of the design, quickly running down the channels and filling the star.

The next cut removed its bonds, and strong hands ripped hip joints from socket. One more violent twist turned its head around. Placed upon its back in the center of the star, its eyes stared forward at the pool. Those eyes were necessary, a seeing force into another realm, eager to find and reveal hidden secrets. One more cut was needed, though, and the captain's blade drew an arcing line beneath its breastbone. The animal's heart beat within.

Thomas brought it, warm and faintly beating to his mouth, and hungrily took bite after bite. "One with this beast," he muttered as he chewed, unfeeling the blood dripping down his cheeks. He consumed it, his soul eagerly devouring though his stomach retched against the metallic taste. The eyes of the animal would soon become his own. There was only one more piece of the spell.

Smiling, and satisfied with his work, Thomas Tew drew out a waterskin, the kind the natives drank from in the Indies. Sealed tightly, it contained the final charm. Reaching in, he grabbed ahold of an object, sacred and still somehow warm despite its removal earlier that night. Though it no longer beat, he felt the pulsing screams of the donor. She had been a prostitute, no one of importance, not even a friend to Ann Mason despite she had made their introduction. He drew forth the human heart, placing it carefully into the void he had made inside the goat, chanting the words the voodoo witches had taught him.

It resumed beating at once, filled with power fueled by the other realm, and his vision changed abruptly.

Thomas Tew saw from two places at once, overlapped as he stood and stared out over the pool. He saw it from above and beside simultaneously, looking deep into the rocks and through them. The double image revealed the secret, as a light glowed from the other side, revealed in the eyes of the goat. Golden coins, forged by Dees with voodoo witchcraft for Queen Elizabeth, then hexed by Le Sage to lift their intended limitations. They had once more been altered and regained their intended form. Captain Tew had found the cavern he sought but was no closer to his treasure. He still needed the passage.

Voices echoed from above, sending him scrambling up the incline and peering into the cave. Bobbing light revealed someone approaching, a man and two women, by the sound of it. He was trapped, found by the coven Rose Sadler had spoken of. Holding his blade aloft, the captain stood ready to run them through no matter their number. Only three, but there would follow more, for sure. He ducked behind some rocks, wishing he had not left the torches burning as they were.

"It's about time she brought her girl into our secrets, but tonight was short notice for a meeting," the man's voice echoed.

"Yes, past time, but timely enough since we've lost Rose and Margaret," a woman replied.

"We need to lie low, until the townsfolk are no longer looking for witches in every corner!" the man suggested. "We tell Elizabeth tonight. We won't be meeting like this for a while or more!"

Tew leaned against the rock wall. *I can kill all three*, he knew. But with his ghostly vision intact, he had another idea. *I will be able to watch their ritual. Let them come and have it, to reveal to me their hiding place.*

Sheathing his blade, the captain picked up a rock, just in case he might be discovered.

First the women emerged, wearing hooded cloaks, followed by a man dressed alike. None saw Tew leaning against the wall with rock in hand and waiting. But one of the women saw the torches and ritual. She let out a scream and the man drew a blade in reaction, leaning over to see what was the matter.

Tew's hand came down swiftly, striking the man in the temple and sending him rolling down the incline. The other woman, who wasn't screaming, turned to face the attacker, but Thomas had anticipated, pulling on her cloak and twisting it over her eyes. After a shove, she tumbled after the man.

Grinning, Captain Tew raced from the cave, still seeing through the lifeless eyes of the goat. In the passageway he froze, footsteps stomping hard toward him. He watched as a large man, muscled by years of farming, came slowly closer. Thomas' hand drew his blade, but it proved unnecessary, as Farmer Griggs passed by without even a glance in his direction.

Those eyes, the captain realized, *lack a soul!* He chuckled, hurrying from the cave and climbing the rocky ledge to find a good hiding place. Not long after, two women, hooded and cloaked like the first pair, hurried the way he had come.

Tew trembled with cold as his goat vision took over, watching the cavern as the large farmer splashed into the pool. Without wasting time or even looking at the injured man, he dove into its depths. Soon the women came into view, and they knelt to help the man. His hood fell away and the captain recognized Constable Cooke. The captain nearly laughed at the thought of the sheriff as a witch.

Two boys, one holding an extinguished torch, quickly followed the two women, making their way down the rocky ledge to follow the way the women had passed. This interested Tew, wondering if one of them was the Mayes boy Ann had told him about. He moved closer, straining to hear their whispered conversation but unable over the wind. What he did witness, was one of them handing the torch off to the other, who scrambled up the rocks and past the captain.

"You!" Tew called out, certain the other would not hear.

The boy froze in his tracks, turning wide-eyed and terrified he had been caught.

"Are you William Mayes?"

"Yuh... Yes, sir!" the boy stammered.

"Good lad." He pointed at the torch. "Are you headed to the Grigg's farm with that?"

The boy finally gained his composure, standing straighter and more like a man. "Who wants to know?" he demanded.

Good, he's got some backbone, Tew thought. "I'm Captain Thomas Tew of *Amity,* that's who wants to know! Now hand it over!" The boy did, and Thomas drew out matches, lighting the torch and shoving it back into the boy's hands. As light flickered across his face, it beamed with awe. "Let's go," Tew commanded, and led the boy to the farm.

McLain was already there, ransacking the home. "We came in as soon as the women left," he explained. "So far there ain't nothin'!"

"I said to look *under* the house! Did you check the root cellar?"

"Aye, Captain, but all that's down there is food and stores. Nothin' out of the ordinary."

"I can find it," the boy offered.

"Oh, can you?" McLain laughed hard, so hard he doubled over.

Mayes snatched the lantern from the man's hand and shoved the torch against his chest. "Yes, I can."

McLain lunged at him, but Tew held up a hand. "I'll go with you. Lead the way, boy."

"If I find it, sir?" the boy asked, "can I be part of the crew?"

"I'll think about it. Now go!" Tew took a moment to peer into the cave, focusing through the lifeless eyes of the goat. Three women knelt over the unconscious man, chanting a healing spell of some sort. Through the ears of the animal it almost sounded Gaelic. The man stirred and began to stand.

The root cellar door opened easily, and Tew and Mayes ducked inside. The lantern, just as McLain said, revealed nothing out of the ordinary. Only shelves and bins of food items and cider. Several stacks of wheeled cheese lined the far wall.

"Well they won't starve anytime soon," the captain remarked. "They're as well stocked as *Amity!*"

The boy, if he heard, said nothing. He merely walked around, holding the lantern close to the ground.

"It certainly ain't buried," Tew pointed out. "They wouldn't have time. It's gonna be behind these shelves."

"No. Those are dusty. This time of year there's no need for pulling jars, and they won't be adding to them till after harvest. Nothing's been touched."

"The sweet potatoes then?"

"No, sir. Those would take too much time to move out of the way and would be a hassle." He carried the lantern to the far wall. "I'm guessing one of the bedrooms is above us, here." Holding it once more to the ground, he smiled. "Here! They rolled away these wheels of cheese, recently! See how the dirt's grooved? There're more footprints here, as well."

"Good job, boy!" Tew praised. "Now find the hidden compartment."

It didn't take William long. He searched along the wall until he found an area recently rubbed free of dust. He pushed and pulled, finally finding a sweet spot that unclasped a latch. The door swung open and he held the light inside. Two chests awaited inspection by the captain.

"Great job, boy!" Tew scrambled in, lifting the lid on one and looking inside. It was filled with a variety of coins and jewels. The next one proved just as bountiful, and he quickly ran to the doorway and called for some crewmen to help. "Haul these to *Amity*!" he commanded.

"What about me, Captain?" William asked. "Can I join the crew?"

"We'll see. I've still got one more chest to find." Stepping out into the night, he ordered McLain, "Take everything of value, then torch the house. Leave the barn, I don't want them *completely* homeless, just our tracks covered."

"Aye, sir," the first mate replied, glaring at a smiling William Mayes.

Tew froze, his double vision blurring then becoming stronger in the cave. A man stepped out of the pool, splashing into the cavern and carrying something in his fist. The girl stepped forward, her right foot nearly smudging the blood of the pentagram. She seemed not to notice she stood in the apex of the star. Tew could barely see the pool around her foot mere inches away.

The mother stepped up, handing her husband a cloak and then whispered in her daughter's ear.

The girl held the coins against her eyes as if seeing through them, chanting the words her mother told her. "Atropos, Clotho, and Lachesis! I am your servant, a slave to the fates and blind to your secrets. Reveal them now. Show unto me the lessons from Manann." At first nothing happened, but then the girl gasped. "I see it, Mother! It's happening as you promised!"

"What do the fates show you, Daughter? Tell us, now, as you see!"

Tew laughed so loudly the men all turned to marvel at what must have appeared to them as madness. *The stupid girl,* he realized, *is standing in my hex! This fate she sees is blended with my spell!*

"I... I do not marry, not Curtis Charles or *any* man! I'm a spinster in a home... a special *kind* of home for those who've lost their wits!" Mary began to tremble, her fingers shaking as she held the coins to her eyes.

Thomas looked up as McLain dragged the torch across the thatch. It lit up at once, a tinderbox thirsty for flame. He tossed it aside and, within seconds, the building was engulfed by a howling inferno.

"I see... fire! Flames as high as treetops! Oh, Mother, it's our home! Our house burns as we speak!"

"Hurry, boys!" Tew commanded his crewmen. They had loaded the wagon, but stood around watching the fire. "Get aboard and let's go! Get back to the ship!" he ordered. He turned to go, but had another thought. Picking the torch off the ground he flung it toward the barn, too. *This will slow them,* he thought, *and ensure our getaway.*

"Our fortune is taken," the girl moaned, "stolen by he who started the fire!"

"Calm, child. Since you've seen this fate there's time to prepare and change it. When does the fire occur?"

The girl let out a whimper, dropping the coins. They bounced and rolled on the rocks, one of them disappearing into the water. The girl dropped to her knees and let out a wailing cry. "Now, Mother! The fire burns *now!*"

Thomas Tew shoved the boy, William, onto the wagon and jumped aboard himself. With the flick of reigns, they lurched into the night, headed for the docks and *Amity*. He finally knew where the Ferryman's coins would be found and how to get there. Now he needed a way to get them out.

The cave was empty now, the occupants having fled to try and save their farm. He was about to sever the connection when a boy stepped to the water's edge, the young man whose torch William had taken. He bent down, picked up two coins from the water and placed them into his pocket. Then he waded out into the pool, diving down and disappearing in its depths. It was several minutes before he emerged, panting and gasping with an ancient chest clutched to his chest.

As he emerged on dry land, he drew out two coins from the chest, holding them to his eyes as he had seen the girl do. He sat there, marveling for many minutes more before pulling them away with a gasp. Setting them aside he drew out the girl's, looking through them in the same way. This time something snapped within him, and he pulled them away. His eyes had changed, nearly as vacant as Josiah Griggs' had been.

Stupid boy, Tew thought. *You can't look through another person's coins!*

The boy must have realized that, because he tucked them back into his pocket and stood, heaving the chest to leave. He paused then glanced at the pool, realizing the girl would return for her coins. Now confused, he couldn't remember which pair was hers and which was his. But Tew knew and watched the idiot toss his own coins into the water.

Thomas Tew laughed once more, but abruptly stopped and turned somber. He needed another plan and only had hours with which to formulate one.

That girl, he realized, *is in for a horrifying experience.* So might another girl, a certain tavern maid whose loyalties he had to test. *I'll send her in the morning to watch and see how truthful she is.*

CHAPTER SIXTEEN

William Mayes sat across from Captain Tew eating his breakfast in the White Horse. Behind the bar, the boy's father watched his son with the pirate, staring disapprovingly, but what could he do? He'd be gutted alive if he forbade this man from befriending his son. He couldn't stop him if he tried. He knew William yearned for adventure and was of age to make his own decision. His scowl from the bar let William know it was time to cut ties with home and sail away. The ship was loaded, provisioned, and manned, so why were they sitting here eating breakfast.

The pirate seemed odd in many other ways on this morning. Eerily cheery, the man was nothing like the night before when William would have described him as a wicked and ill-disposed cur. Instead of ranting and raving or barking orders, he had spent most of the morning staring off into space. It was as if the man were somewhere else entirely.

"It's time to go," the pirate finally said.

"To set sail?" William asked excitedly.

"To confront your friend, that Curtis Charles fellow," Tew corrected.

"Oh. What has he done we need to confront?"

"He's stolen something of mine, has it hid in his apartment."

"How do you know this?"

"I know," the pirate said, suddenly resembling the man from the night before. "That's all *you* need to know." He stood, noticeably failing to pay for his breakfast and made his way to the door.

William hurried to keep up, shooting his father an apologetic glance. The tavern keeper refused to meet his eyes and that hurt the young man deeply. He found himself torn in that moment, yearning to run to his father and continue working the tavern, or to follow this adventurer and bring back gold and jewels the next time he returned to Newport. He chose the latter, catching the door before it closed and moving quickly to walk beside the captain.

"Am I part of your crew now, Captain Tew?"

"Crew?" The man, no longer distant-eyed, hissed his response. "You ain't earned nothin', yet."

"What do I need to do?" William pleaded. He wanted nothing more in this moment than to hire on, join this man, and sail the Round. So many riches awaited him, and the prospect of killing Moghuls did not bother him in the least. "I'm an experienced sailor, sailed with William Kidd, I did!"

"So I heard."

"I'd be valuable to you, as an officer, even. I'm learned and can do figures."

Tew paused, eyeing someone coming up the other end of the street. It was mostly empty, this early in the morning, and the woman was easy to spot.

William squinted his eyes to see farther, recognizing Ann Mason. She looked a frightful mess instead of her usual beauty. Her hair, usually fluffed, powdered, and styled, hung wet against her face and clung sodden on her damp shoulders. Her entire dress clung to her body, as if she had walked out of the ocean itself.

Tew laughed at the sight, roaring with pleasure but oddly not from surprise. It seemed as if he expected her to be soaked to the bone.

"What did you find?" he asked.

"Nothing," the girl replied, then reconsidered. "Well, I found the second cavern, but no chest of coins. The girl had no idea it was missing and no inkling where it's gone."

"That's all? How'd you get her to show you the hiding place?" he demanded, still smiling as if holding a dark secret only he knew.

"I offered her a trade. Said I knew where to find her family's treasure and offered to give it up for the coins."

"Oh?" Tew asked, surprised. "That's all? No mention of *me*?"

"Of course not! You know I'd never brag about knowing you, much less that you took her family's gold!"

Tew pointed at William. "You told *him* about our dalliances. His friend, too."

"Only to gain their aid, I swear!" She came across defiant, but the look on her face betrayed fear—both of the man and what he'd do if he caught her in a bigger lie. "Besides, William's father *owns* the tavern! He knows we've met because his father always complains about you being there!"

Tew calmed his demeanor. "So the lass has no idea *I've* got her gold or that it's loaded on *Amity*?"

"None at all," Ann insisted.

"William," Tew suddenly said, shifting focus to the boy. "Where's your friend Curtis Charles reside?"

"Nuh... Not far, sir! Just down this way!" William led the pair past the inn, to a small apartment on its own. It belonged to Curtis's father, the ferryman, before his accident. He pointed at the door, stepping aside so the captain could do his work.

"Well?" the captain demanded.

"Well what, sir?"

"What'cha gonna do to *him* when we find him with my treasure?" Tew asked.

"Sir?" William didn't like the suggestion. Curtis was his friend, his *only* friend in Newport and wanted no harm to befall him.

"If'n we find my coins, you will prove you're worth by beating your friend."

"Sir? What would that accomplish? You'll have your gold!"

Tew's face abruptly grew meaner, his eyes drilling into William's soul. "That's not what I commanded. Will you prove your loyalty or not?"

"Aye, sir!" William promised, suddenly praying to God they never found the coins. "But please wait over there, he can't see me with you or he'll never talk!"

"Knock on the door!" the captain growled, stepping out of sight.

William did, shouting as he did when no one answered right away. "Curtis!" he announced, "It's me, William!"

At first no sounds came from within, but then the door inched open and Curtis Charles stood blinking against the sunlight. He was a mess, smelling like a mixture between a brewery and a stable floor.

"Judas, Curtis!" William exclaimed, covering his nose at the smell. "You smell like you slept with swine!"

"I had a long night," was all his friend replied. "Where did you go? How come you never returned?"

William ignored the questions, feeling urgency in the way Tew's eyes watched from his left. "What did you see, after I left?"

"I saw some things, not a lot," Curtis said with a shrug. He was hiding something; William could tell by his eyes. But then, he quickly added, "But they're witches for sure."

"I knew it!"

Curtis frowned, as if remembering more of the night. "You left me on my own, William. Why?"

"I had to. I ran into some friends and they... well, they had other plans for my night."

"I don't understand," Curtis frowned, mulling over thoughts. Suddenly he exclaimed, "*You* burned her farm! With *my* torch and she'll blame *me*!"

"How did you…" But William felt Tew's presence even stronger, as if saying, *Prove my loyalty!* Standing taller, the young man declared, "Aye, I burned it, that's the only way to deal with witches!"

"You said you were bringing help!" Curtis protested.

"He did," Tew shouted, pushing the door completely open. "And here they are now." Curtis Charles recoiled at the sight of Thomas Tew. "Enough pleasantries," the captain growled. "Does he have it or not?"

"I was working up to that, Thomas!" William replied angrily. "I asked you to wait."

"I wait for no man. The call to sea and lure of great account is too great to resist," the pirate barked. "Let's finish here and get back to the Pirate's Round!"

William, emboldened by what was promised, made up his mind to earn his spot on the crew. He abruptly threw a punch at Curtis, striking his jaw and knocking his friend to the floor.

"What did you see?" he demanded. "Did the witches reveal the whereabouts of the coins?"

"Wuh… what coins?" William knew when his friend was lying and kicked him hard. "He has 'em then," William decided, kicking several more times. "Where'd you stash 'em?" he demanded.

"Wasted energy," Ann proclaimed, pushing her way into the room. "He's only got *one* place to *hide 'em*!" She opened the closet door and all eyes fell upon the chest, uncovered, and hastily pushed behind the door.

"Great mother of fortune!" Thomas Tew exclaimed, falling to his knees and flipping open the lid. "It's them! Dee's cursed treasure!" He turned to William. "This *is* enough payment, William Mayes, enough to earn your spot on my crew!"

"So the honor's mine? Officer's title without strings?" William demanded.

"Aye. Full and without strings. You can keep some of the gold we recovered last night, as well. Consider it an investment in your future."

"Thank you, Captain. When do we leave for the Arabian Sea?"

"Tonight," Tew said with a smile. "I've got what I came for, and now it's time to plunder the Mughal Convoy!"

"That's mine," Curtis Charles accused, surprising himself with his boldness. "You won't be leaving with it."

William's kick took him in the ribs, shattering two. "We take what we want, coward. And you *won't* follow, and do you know why?" He feigned crying and rubbed his eyes. "Because you're a sniveling son of a ferryman, a washed-up, terrified child afraid of the sea."

"Ah," said Tew, "don't treat the child so!" He walked over and tossed two coins on the floor beside Curtis. "Here's your share of the treasure, boy. Two coins. Two. That's all you get from Thomas *Tew*!" He roared laughter and joined William in breaking more ribs and bruising Curtis's skin.

"That's enough," Ann pleaded, suddenly feeling sorry for the boy. "Let him be!"

Tew turned, his eyes full of merriment. "Enough?" Looking down at the boy he smiled broadly. "No, not *nearly* enough." He motioned for William to help heave Curtis onto the bed, laying him prone with arms by his side. Picking the coins off the floor he carefully placed them over two unconscious eyes. "You'll see a different future now, through those, once I'm done with 'em."

"What will you do?" William asked, confused. He suddenly felt sorry for how he had beaten his friend, horrified by the way he had enjoyed the rampage.

"Move that table," Tew commanded. He drew out a waterskin, untied the top, and began drawing a symbol on the ground.

William nearly retched when he saw blood instead of water leave the skin, suddenly worried about the company he kept. But he complied, then watched with curiosity as the captain drew a five-pointed star. "What's that?" he asked.

"Shut up," Tew growled, placing the chest of coins at the tip of the star.

William fell silent, curious by the ritual, but gripped by fear. As realization set in, so did regret. *What's he gonna to do to Curtis?* he wondered. He felt at a small knife on his belt. It was for scaling fish, but might do on a man. But the broad blade on the captain's hip would do more damage to him, so he stashed any ideas of violence aside.

Tew began to chant in a strange language. It was almost Latin, as William had heard from the Catholics up the way, but eerily different. There were also undertones of a different language, several in fact, unlike any he had ever heard.

Ann seemed confused as well, moving next to William and holding tightly onto his arm. "It's witchcraft," she muttered.

"No," Tew said, turning slowly to face the pair. "It's something far stronger, from down in Xaymaca, the land of wood and water. The Africans brought it, twisting it together with arts of their own to form a pure magic, one so powerful it overcomes the gods themselves."

Next to William, Ann tensed, gripping his arm tighter and moving behind him. "You're scaring me, Thomas."

The captain ignored them both and their worries, continuing as if what he performed were normal or even godly. "The ignorant call it voodoo, but it's much, much simpler than that." He stepped forward, moving between the pair and the door.

William's hand once more found the handle of his scaling knife, gripping it as tightly as Ann held his arm.

"This ritual is simple and will return the queen's coins to the state Captain Le Sage intended."

"What will that do to Curtis Charles?" William demanded. "How's he to be involved?"

"Your dear friend will be locked into a deep sleep for a time, wandering between realms and lost in the fate he discovers in the coins." Tew explained. "It's a blessing, really, giving him a chance to make something of himself. See? I'm not a *complete* monster."

Thomas moved closer to Ann, his lips close to hers, teasing a kiss.

She relaxed some and giving in relieved he meant no harm. Softly responding to his advance, she softened her mouth to meet his.

"Why did you do it?" he asked her quietly, whispering like a lover into her ear.

"Do what?" she asked, unsure of his meaning.

"Why'd you lie to me?" As soon as the captain spoke his hand flashed, drawing his blade and ramming it deep into Ann's belly, breaking skin just below the breastbone, careful not to damage the heart just above. "I *heard* you tell that bitch I have her gold. Her family will come after me now unless I do deal with you as a warning!"

The woman's eyes screamed silence into the room, round and shocked, but not at all surprised by the evil that ended her life. She had danced with the devil called Captain Tew and now only served one purpose—to taint the gold with her treacherous past of lies.

William tried to make for the door.

"Avast!" the pirate called, freezing the boy in his tracks. "Take two coins from the chest," Tew commanded. "Bring them to me!"

William obeyed, feeling around with shaky hands and drawing out two pieces of Ferryman gold, listening as Tew condemned the woman, laying her softly into the middle of the pentagram.

"The coins drawn from the water's edge were touched by both the girl and mother," he explained to the dying woman, "and so they're useful. With them I can forge lies, masking your betrayal and ensuring madness takes root in her. This is your penance for transgression, to condemn that child to a life of confusion, one that hides my role in the arson." With surgical precision, he carefully sliced a line beneath her breasts. "Good girl," he said into her staring eyes, "I need it beating."

To William's surprise, she nodded wordlessly her understanding.

"Hurry with those coins and place them over her eyes." A reached hand wriggled into the space, finding the organ, and ripping it free.

The woman gasped, eyes alive for one haunting moment in which they met William's. They pleaded for his help, but what could he do? Then they blinked twice, sadly staring through two pieces of gold.

"It's done," Thomas Tew finally announced. "Now take those coins and swap them for those in his pocket."

William found his hands comply, rummaging through his friend's clothing like a common thief. He found a purse and drew it forth, marveling at the laughing skulls within.

"Good. Now place them under her tongue. Let those be her passage. These," he pointed to her eyes, "must go where you found the others."

Again, William followed his captain's dark orders, taking the coins from Ann and placing them with Curtis Charles. The man slumbered so soundly, waking him was no longer an option.

"What happens now?" he asked quietly, accomplice to the damned. "Won't the constable wonder at the coins when they're found?"

"Not at all. He's part of the mystic coven and will think these coins belong to Ann. She'll be buried with them as fare for their fabled Ferryman."

"But her death! The ritual! Won't he investigate?"

"Investigate *what*?" Tew asked with roaring laughter. "Your friend will be blamed for it all, both the arson and the stolen gold." He pointed at the pentagram, "And the rituals. Constable Cooke will burn him at the stake or, with a bit of luck, let the townspeople bear that duty."

"What now, Captain? Do we simply sail away?"

"Aye, but first we have one more thing to do. In the center of town, they keep a pyre ready to light, one to discourage witches like Rose Sadler and the others already condemned. I'll finish this ritual by placing this heart beneath the stack. If I'm correct, Mary Griggs will take Ann's coins from his pocket, confusing her visions thinking they were hers not this girl's damnation. This heart," he said as he placed it into the waterskin, "will burn with your friend and seal his fate as one stuck between the realms."

William nodded grimly. He had no choice but to follow this man, his soul now condemned for the part he played. Head down, he followed his captain from the apartment and toward the town square. If they hurried, no one would see them place the organ where his friend would soon be committed to purgatory.

PART IV
THE FERRYMAN

CHAPTER SEVENTEEN

Constable Cooke, fed up with the past forty-eight hours and nursing a slight headache from it all, stepped into his office. His feet froze as soon as he did. Both his deputies fussed over the body on the table. It stank to high heaven, charred like an overcooked rat thrown into the fire with hair and all. Without any regard for the dead, they dug at the boy's eyes—or rather the sockets where eyes once set, trying to pry out the golden coins.

"Stop that at *once*!" he cried, more out of fear for what would happen than for respect for the corpse. But his meaning did not affect the tone, which wasn't lost on the men. They stepped back, startled by his sudden ferocity, and waited.

He stumbled for a moment, then said what they expected, "Don't you have any respect for the dead?"

"Well, he don't need 'em, and we do!" Jasper Constance replied defiantly.

"You... do?" Finneas asked deliberately, a tone of anger reflected in his words. "Don't I *pay* you enough?"

"No, sir! I mean, yes, sir!" the deputy argued.

"Get out of here, the *both* of you!" Cooke ordered, sending the pair running for the door. "Don't return till you know decency!"

They wouldn't. Neither had that compassion.

Finneas stared down at the boy.

He was cooked as well as a Christmas goose, only worse. There was nothing left to this corpse, except for the harder tissues which fused to the bones.

It's not Curtis Charles' fault. No. Not in the least. Wrong place at the wrong time, the constable reasoned, *was his sin.* He had known the boy's father, ridden his ferry even, and viewed him wearing similar wrappings—only white instead of black. White was for a pure death, acceptable to God. The sight of the black shroud around the boy chilled the constable. It was added after they pulled the charred remains from the stake. White wasn't appropriate in this case, not for witches burned so...

Witches. Finneas laughed at the thought, breathing in a bit of the filth floating around the body. A brief gag became a coughing fit and, once it subsided, he finished his thought. Witches were just people like him, of an *alternative* belief. What were they hurting? *The church would never understand,* he knew, *nor forgive.*

So was the way with Rhode Island and the northern colonies. No matter what dissention Roger Williams had, or how tolerable he claimed to be for all religions, there would never be a place in which mysticism was safe from persecution. Salem had proven that just two years prior.

"Look what mess you got yourself into," he said to the body of Curtis Charles, leaning over it and staring into the coins. "All you had to do was leave well enough alone, but you had to push, didn't you? Where's the queen's coins, boy? Where'd you hide them? He's got 'em, doesn't he? That cursed Thomas Tew."

He felt at a pouch around his neck, a pair of coins tucked within and matching the boy's eyes.

"I guess you saw your future, then, didn't you? And now it's your vision for eternity. I've seen mine as well," Cooke explained. "That's how I became constable. It was the only way to protect our coven. I hate it though, this responsibility, and wish I could do something else. Sometimes it ain't all that satisfying knowing you're locked forever to one thing—ain't no hope in that. At least I've seen my death. Well, the how if not the when."

The body of Curtis Charles stared back disinterested, but staring intently as if listening to his words, so he continued. It was nice admitting all this to someone, even a dead man bound to carry his secrets to hell.

"It'll be my ticker that gives out, suddenly and without warning, when I go. I've already felt the pain, so I know I'll recognize it. It doesn't last long though, just enough to leave me lying about thinking about how much I hate being bound to this job."

He glanced at the door, yearning to walk away right then and there. He and Sally could pack their things, they had plenty coin saved up, and catch a ship headed south to Virginia. Or they could venture west to William Penn's colony. Those Quakers were even more tolerant than Roger Williams. But, in the end, they were still Quakers, an obscenely blasphemous bunch who threw themselves into fits of foolery.

Answer... a voice said in his mind.

Finneas paused, unsure of what he had just heard.

Answer, the voice demanded.

"Answer what?" he asked the room, eyes glued to the face of Curtis Charles.

The voice spoke again, more clearly this time, distinctly into his mind. It said,

Atropos, Clotho, and I am the big brother.
Listen to my Servant, and you might not suffer.
Tread carefully around the ferry,
As he holds your obituary,
Though I seem to wind and wander,
There are lessons in the water.
His duty is to ferry you,
Oarless and without an answer to the end.

Finneas suddenly feared he was going mad, terrified by the horrific ringing now plaguing his ears. "I... I don't understand," he admitted. "What does this mean?" Staring down at the queen's coins though, he realized. "You're the Ferryman?"

Wrong answer, the voice told him.

Finneas Cooke fell backward, his chest feeling as if it were suddenly kicked by a mule. The entire left side of his neck felt numb, taking with it his entire arm on that side. He began to sweat profusely, filled with panic as he recognized what was happening.

He staggered, falling backward against the wall. His eyes, once wide and full of life turned lifeless, and he slumped down the wall to rest uselessly on the floor.

Elizabeth and Josiah Griggs led Mary down the pier. Providence was a much larger town than Newport, very nearly a city like Boston or New York. People bustled here and there, dashing off on their errands whatever they may be. Elizabeth had to cling to her husband several times as carters rolled out, heedless of pedestrians in their way.

"We'll be trampled," Elizabeth decided. "No one here cares about anyone else!"

"We don't have coin for a wagon," her husband replied. "What we got from the sale of Castle Hills will barely pay for our establishment here."

The mother shot her daughter an irritated look. Half the girl's hair was gone by now, ripped free of its bleeding roots. She had a fistful of it in her mouth, chewing as she walked. Once, Elizabeth would have demanded she stop, but no longer. The girl's mind was gone, spent by madness. *Who cares how these staring eyes judge us as parents, failures for rearing this lunatic instead of a woman?*

They found the boarding house without trouble, a two story establishment run by a Baptist preacher named James Brown. The family owned several industries, including an iron works and a distillery of rum. Mr. Brown had already hired Josiah on at the foundry and offered to help Elizabeth secure employment at a nearby textile shop.

His wife, also named Mary, had taken to their daughter right away. She would serve as her governess and nurse.

"There's only the matter of board, then, Mr. Griggs," the pastor reminded.

"Yes, sir," Josiah agreed, pulling an envelope from his breast pocket. "Without a structure on the land, we could only sell Castle Hills for a fraction of what it's worth. But there's enough there to pay for three years of care as we agreed. The rest goes toward that plot of land on which we agreed I'll build our own place."

"Excellent. I'll have the title drawn up. But what about after three years has passed? What arrangement will we make then?"

"We'll pay monthly for her to reside here as a tenant under your wife's tutelage, Elder Brown." Elizabeth conceded. "At whatever rate you deem fair."

"Yes, that does seem the best arrangement," the pastor agreed. He and his wife also recognized that the Griggs were unfit as parents. "What if you... and please forgive me, but *all* things are possible under God's eye, but what if either or both of you meet an untimely demise from either illness or accident?"

"There's a clause in our wills naming you as her guardian, and our estate, whatever that may be, goes entirely to continue her care."

James Brown nodded then stood with outstretched hand. "Then we have an agreement, sir!"

Elizabeth watched the two Marys getting acquainted in the corner. The older woman seemed perplexed by the younger staring at an empty rocker in the corner.

"What do you see, Mary?" the pastor's wife asked gently.

"She sees my grandmother," Elizabeth explained.

"Oh, she's here, too," Mary said matter of fact, "only not alone. But she *did* say you're a fornicator like your cousin, Mrs. Brown."

"I'm sorry," Elizabeth intervened, rushing to make things right. "This is part of what we discussed, the madness. She sees things that aren't here and says things she doesn't mean."

"No matter, Mrs. Griggs," the woman said with a smile. She had been shaken but kept her composure. "I took no offense and clearly see the source of her confused words."

Elizabeth relaxed and allowed them to continue.

Mary Brown asked, "What did you mean, Mary, when you mentioned my cousin? I have many. Of which do you know?" the pastor's wife asked.

"Curtis Charles says you're a Harris, but your grandmother was one of those good for nothing Tew. Your cousin, Thomas, is sailing toward his death as we speak, he said. A horrible one, at that!"

Every adult in the room stiffened at her words, then turned their eyes toward the rocker in the corner. They each could nearly hear the cackle of laughter as it began to rock slowly back and forth. Elizabeth could swear that she saw two golden eyes staring back at her.

Mary Brown abruptly screamed and everyone's attention returned to Mary. The girl had somehow picked up a letter opener from the desk, holding it firmly against her own left eye. While the adults had been watching the chair, she had already punctured the right one. It oozed with jelly streaming down her face, appearing like a trail of tears slowed by the passage of time.

Josiah moved in, meaning to wrench it from his daughter's hand but arrived too late. Elizabeth retched as her daughter violently removed her gift of sight.

"Why?" Josiah asked, pulling the object free and hugging his daughter closely. "Why did you do this? Now you'll *never* be the same!"

"The Ferryman comes for us, Father," she explained pleasantly, "and I answered his riddle wrongly. He was innocent and we wronged him! Now I'm not fit to see him coming."

CHAPTER EIGHTEEN

Desert winds warmed the night, steamy and without giving respite from the day's heat. It lingered, heavy and dry while the crew tossed and turned below decks. Only a few men stood topside, William Mayes and Thomas Tew among them, watching the Mandab Strait and any ships trying to make their way in or out. They expected the convoy, more than twenty ships laden heavily with gems and gold, tribute for the Moghul Emperor.

Other pirates lurked nearby, but *Amity* was first in the strait. Tew promised his men first choice of bounty, choosing as his target one of the Ganjah dhows.

"Surely they haven't slipped by us in the night?" Tew growled to Mayes.

"I don't believe so, Captain, but our eyes are peeled and the moon nearly full. We'll see them, sir."

Both men continued their watch, peering across the sea and looking for the moonlight reflection on sails.

"There," Tew finally muttered, spotting a shadow upon the horizon, "keeping close to the western shore. Do you see it?"

"No, I..." At first William did not, but soon he caught glimpse of the shimmering patch of darkness just above the horizon. It was a line of them, a convoy of ships passing in the dark. "It's them, the convoy, Captain! You've found it!"

"Shake the crew and rouse them as fighting men!" Tew commanded. "Keep them quiet and we'll take her by surprise! If'n we can barely see them, p'haps they don't see us at all!"

William nodded, hurrying below decks and sounding the alarm.

Eager men sprang from their hammocks, the night's sweat no longer a burden while cool riches waited. Knives and cutlasses were chosen, as desirous of blood as the men were for gold, silver, and jewels. The veteran fighters remembered the first Ganjah dhow the captain had delivered, teeming with rewards after striking its colors without a fight. The rookies hoped he would do the same, and every hand rushed topside to join the fray.

William felt their excitement rush through him, finding it difficult not to let it become his own. This was, after all, why he had joined the devil's crew, to return to Newport as much more than the son of a tavern owner. He planned to return wealthy, dressed in finery like Tew and able to buy up the entire town. *I'll be mayor, someday, or even governor,* the boy mused. He drew his own blade from its sheath on his hip and eyed his reflection in the steel.

His eyes caused him to pause, briefly thinking of poor Curtis Charles back home. Those eyes had pleaded for mercy while they beat him, and he would see more like the boy aboard the Ganjah dhow. William swallowed guiltily at this part of his chosen profession, but he was a pirate, and pirates showed no mercy.

Racing topside, he joined captain and crew.

The deck was a flurry of activity, with sailors climbing the rigging above, and gunners ready to fire and reload below. All three masts unfurled at once, and the sloop of war lunged forward, racing toward the line of ships sneaking by.

"That one," Tew commanded the gunnery officer, then turned to William. "Ensign Mayes, ready the away team. You're swinging on the grappling crew!"

William felt a lump lodge in his throat. Other than Curtis Charles, he had never harmed a hair on anybody, much less lead a band of killers onto another vessel. *Will I freeze?* he wondered, suddenly worrying there might be something, anything, worse than freezing. He steadied his nerves, readying them to be called upon. *They're only Moghuls,* he told himself, *akin to savages some of the veterans say.* But he knew they made that claim to better palate the slaughter, and knowing that did little to stay his anxiety.

"Ready portside guns," Tew ordered. "We'll turn hard to starboard once we've come alongside."

A thought struck William. *That will open up our broadside to their guns, as well.* "Captain," he asked, "what if they fire upon *us?*"

"They won't," snapped Tew.

"How do you..."

"The thing about these convoy is they *never* fight back! That's the whole secret of the Pirate's Round. We come, they cower, and we plunder!"

But William spotted movement on the other ship. "Sir," he protested, "they..." But it was too late, and several guns roared into the night. The one he had been watching, *Fateh Muhammed,* flashed muzzles toward *Amity* and meant to fight.

Splinters flew as shot hit home, ripping timbers to pieces and sending men ducking for cover. All except the captain, who stood defiant, staring down his rival and grinding his teeth with anger.

"Fire portside!" Tew screamed. *Amity* responded with far superior firepower, severely damaging the dhow.

William watched his captain's eyes, expectantly darting upward at the enemy's mast. *He still expects them to strike colors!* he realized, biting his lip in sudden fear. There *would* be a fight.

As soon as *Amity* fired, several of the other dhows broke formation, pulling away from the convoy and moving to encircle the pirate vessel. They crawled with armed marauders, each waving scimitars or kneeling to aim muskets.

"There's hundreds of them, Captain!" William tried to warn.

"Then prepare to fight them off!" Tew screamed, his spit striking William's cheek. "They're only mercenaries and won't have the stomach for our cannons!" Turning to the gunnery officer, he added, "Fire full starboard, then at will from every gun! Keep them off our rails!"

The man nodded, then relayed the order.

The closest starboard enemy met the blast head on, ripping apart the forecastle and forward mast. It turned hard to port, its own guns pointed at *Amity*.

William Mayes was no longer anxious about the battle, he was terrified. Looking around, he saw similar feelings expressed on *Amity's* crew. Captain Tew was not prepared for this campaign, especially not this engagement. He had underestimated Moghul resolve. The only course was to turn tail and run.

"Captain," he offered, pointing to a gap between vessels. "We can make it through there and escape to freedom!"

Tew's expression changed abruptly, from worry to anger, as he faced the young ensign. "I'm no coward! We fight to the man!" By now the entire topside crew watched their leader as well, waiting to hear his words of encouragement. "We came here for *one* dhow, but we'll be leavin' here with three! This is our..."

The turning dhow cut him off, firing its full broadside and striking mostly below the rails. Several balls whisked over the deck.

Thomas Tew had grown silent, his words forgotten and eyes large with shock. They turned downward, toward his belly. While his crewmen watched on with horror, the pirate felt at the mess above his belt, grabbing his dangling entrails and desperately trying to push them back in. A random shot had struck his side, ripping it open and gutting him while standing on the deck. For several seconds, confused fingers fumbled around, intent on making himself whole, but to no avail. He finally collapsed to his knees, staring pleadingly to the ensign for help.

The air around the ship abruptly changed, hanging thicker and heavy. Where once he could smell gunpowder, William's nose found nothing at all. He licked his lips, expecting the salty sweat so prevalent in this hot region, but instead found his senses had either dulled or gone completely. A misty fog rolled in, surrounding the ships with an eerie veil.

Startled by sudden realization, William was confounded by the image before his eyes. Neither ships nor men moved about, frozen in time like unseeing statues. Only he and Captain Tew blinked life in that moment, staring at each other with confused wonder.

"Am I dying?" Tew asked.

"I think you already have," William corrected. "But why I'm with you, I don't understand."

"I can't move," Thomas complained, his arms hanging uselessly at his side. His entrails shriveled as soon as he spoke, decaying and withering into dust on the planks. Had there been any breeze at all, they would have blown the pile asunder.

William tried his own feet, finding they worked to carry him to the rails. "Something's out there," he said, focusing eyes on a single torch emerging from the fog.

As it ventured closer he recognized a ferryboat, much like those used back home. A single pilot stood on the bow, holding the torch with outstretched arm. Unmanned oars moved in and out of the water with a rhythmic effort, propelling the vessel slowly closer until it banged alongside *Amity*.

William shouted down at the pilot, "State your business here!" But the hooded man did not answer, merely waited. His identity was a mystery, with a dark shroud completely hiding his face. "Look at me, sir! Who are you?"

"Perhaps he has come for me," Tew suggested, his pending death obvious. "The Ferryman come to claim his coins."

William turned. "That's ridiculous," he replied, then turned again to shout once more at the newcomer.

The boat was empty.

"He's gone!" William proclaimed, whirling around to find a shrouded specter standing over Thomas Tew. "Back away from him," the ensign commanded, drawing his cutlass and holding it shakily toward the ghoul.

The stranger faced the dying man, croaking a question in a low voice.

"Atropos, Clotho, and I am the big brother.
Listen to my Servant, and you might not suffer.
Tread carefully around the ferry,
As he holds your obituary,
Though I seem to wind and wander,
There are lessons in the water.
His duty is to ferry you,
Oarless and without an answer to the end."

"What are you asking him?" William demanded.

"Answer," the specter demanded of Tew.

"I... I don't know," the terrified man replied.

"Answer..." The shrouded newcomer moved, his back to William while he revealed his face to Thomas. "Answer," he once more commanded.

"It's... a riddle?" William realized, pondering the words.

"Answer..."

Thomas Tew stared up at the specter, his terrified eyes wet with tears. "The Ferryman. You're the Ferryman but I don't understand how! Either way, my passage was paid!"

"Now I ask William Mayes," the specter replied, suddenly standing before the ensign.

William gazed upon the shrouded figure, a frightful face coming into focus a foot or two away from his own. Most of its flesh had been seared, burned permanently away, and that which remained had fused sinew and bone. Where its eyes had once been rounded and full, the Ferryman stared back with laughing gold coins, presumably the same given to him by Thomas Tew.

This can't be Curtis Charles, William marveled, recalling the ritual in the boy's apartment. *Ann's death, had the curse forced him into this fate?*

"Answer!" the Ferryman demanded, leaning closer with breath as hot as fire.

William's nose finally detected a smell, that of brimstone. He stammered as he attempted to solve the riddle, searching his memory for the Greek names the specter had mentioned. He shouted out, "The fates! You are fate! Atropos and Clotho were the younger sisters of Lachesis, who measured a man's worth by his thread of life. You are here to reveal a man's fate and judge the destination of his passage!"

"Correct," the Ferryman replied, his arms suddenly filled with a familiar chest. William recognized it at once, filled with the Ferryman's coins. It was the same Thomas Tew had taken from Curtis Charles. As abruptly as he had come, the specter and the captain disappeared.

William rushed to the rail, watching as the ferryboat rowed out across the water. He wondered for a moment where his former friend would deliver the captain, but the man's lifetime of deception had already ensured his destination.

What now of mine?

Images suddenly rushed into William's mind, of sea adventure and privateering. His fate was laid out then, a string of events leading to fame and fortune. All at once he knew which way to steer his own life, while waiting for the Ferryman to return to claim him in the same fashion as Tew. He and the crew would be captured, rescued in a few months by another pirate, Henry Every. Eventually Mayes would be given a ship to captain, *The Pearl*, relentlessly pursued by the pirate-hunter William Kidd. But fortune *would* be his, returning to Newport a wealthy man. Evading Kidd, he would retire in his father's stead, the proprietor of the White Horse Tavern.

He reached down and felt inside his pocket, touching and fingering two golden coins. They would be his passage when the time came to pay the Ferryman.

CHAPTER NINETEEN

Providence, Rhode Island, 1740

The lunatic rubbed at her bald head, deeply scarred over time. Her fingers, devoid of nails long ago removed by doctors, were clubbed nubs that did no harm. That did not stop her, though, from trying to rub off the filthy stain of witchcraft. She hated the feel of it, that sin she committed, but her mother had forced her to dabble. Though never her intent to stray, the stain had marked her permanently for hell.

The sound of two people entering her room did not lift her attention, there was no reason to look, she could not see. The sound of door closing softly behind them revealed the doctor. He, unlike the orderlies, did not carelessly startle or act roughly toward her. The other person she could not guess an identity, the sound of his shoes were muffled like those of a finer gentleman.

They began to speak to each other, ignoring her, though questions would come. She imagined each of them, one dressed nicely and the other in a white coat and waited pleasantly to be addressed.

"Here we have Mary Griggs," Dr. Dexter explained. "She suffers from hallucinations and dementia, Mr. Locke. She was first brought to us in 1732 upon the death of Elder James Brown. She had been his ward after her parents died in 1696."

"How did her parents pass?" Locke asked.

"Murder suicide. Elizabeth Griggs…"

"Mommy." Mary interrupted with a broad smile aimed where she believed the men stood.

"Elizabeth Griggs killed her husband in some kind of ritual, then went mad, herself. They found her stripped naked in the center of town, rambling about some ferryman and a riddle wrongly answered, then threw herself in front of a coach and its team of charging horses."

"He's coming," Mary insisted, nodding her head vigorously. "The Ferryman comes for all of us!"

Mr. Locke had questions. "Based on my own experience with the insane, I've learned these intellectual disorders are based in the realm of ideas. Her affective state seems focused on this ferryman. Does she mean Charon?"

"No. I mean Curtis Charles," she answered for herself.

Dr. Dexter answered as well. "She *is* centrally focused on the second coming of some supernatural ferryman, and it could be based on the myth and passage to the underworld, but she insists there have been many names for Charon. She mentioned once Manann but has since called him *Curtis Charles*."

"Intriguing," Mr. Locke remarked. "I'd like to study her closely while I'm in Providence."

"Of course! You'll have full access. Now, if you'll come with me we have another patient, a Scottish Lord who raves on and on about voodoo magic from the islands. Claimed his cat is a werewolf or some nonsense. He insists on drawing little dolls on every surface of his cell."

"Intriguing," Mr. Locke said again.

The door once again shut behind the two men.

Mary turned her attention to Curtis Charles sitting beside her. He often came to visit, but never for long. He had proven a good listener and might have turned out a dutiful husband had her fate been different.

"How's Mother and Father?" she asked

Dead...

"Yes, that's nice, isn't it? Such a good state to be in, especially when deceased. I've found that my own state is dismal, locked in this room and unable to scratch free the filth of my mother's sin. Where *is* she now, do you think?"

Dead...

"Yes, such a lovely place this time of year." She reached over to touch his hand, feeling around several times to find it. "Won't you scratch my head for me?" she asked with a hint of flirting. "It itches so badly, and your bony hands are perfect for scratching."

Dead...

"You're so thoughtful," she told him, blowing him a kiss. Suddenly aware he was gone, her ears scanned the room and she called out, "Curtis Charles? Please come back! I want to go with you! I want to visit Mother and Father!"

Your mother and father are sinners, Molly Flannigan's ghost replied cynically from the corner.

Mary recognized she was a ghost, always had, which proved to herself she was not insane.

So are you... the apparition insisted.

"Oh shut up," Mary said. She would have rolled her eyes, but those pesky orbs had been long removed at Curtis Charles' insistence. "I wish you'd go away and leave me alone. I'm perfectly capable of living out my days in silence and without company."

She got her wish, and Molly Flannigan disappeared at once. Unfortunately, she was replaced by Elizabeth Griggs.

You're a horrible daughter, the woman accused.

"You're a despicable mother," Mary argued.

Dead... Curtis Charles whispered, having returned from his errand.

Sinners, Molly Flannigan accused, *all of you!*

CHAPTER TWENTY

Curtis Charles made his way to the White Horse Tavern. He had visited the place many times of late, most notably when claiming William Mayes' father. He had died of natural causes and was buried true to his Irish custom with two coins under his tongue. William Junior, returned from his adventures overseas, had insisted upon it. With passage paid, the righteous soul was delivered to paradise.

This next visit was paid for as well.

He had grown accustomed to death, both his own and others, eternally locked in the space between realms. He was never alone, surrounded by roaming souls. Depression and longing had fled upon death, freeing him from those painful memories of losing his father, and going the way of smell and taste. Oddly, he found he no longer missed those senses only important when a spirit had a body and had use for either taste or smell. To his surprise though, his sight had been altered, seeing the world simultaneously from three different realms. That was a benefit only he enjoyed, given his role in this realm.

In one realm, that of the living, this tavern was full of activity, brimming with song and the spilling of ale. Those celebrants could not see him, of course, and any who might had touched madness or witchcraft. In this realm, a peaceful purgatory for those bound elsewhere, a solitary woman cleaned up after imagined patrons. She hummed a merry tune as she swept, then picked up discarded mugs to wash. Each night was the same for Ann Mason, but always felt like a new experience. Curtis enjoyed seeing her and had often done so out of nostalgia.

As soon as he crossed the threshold, he appeared to her as he had while living. She smiled warmly at his youthful face and warm eyes of blue.

"We're closed, but I'll fill a mug for you, Curtis Charles. What'll you have?"

"Ale, please, Ann. It doesn't have to be in a clean mug."

She laughed at his words, catching his meaning. "No custom of *mine* will ever be served a dirty glass," she insisted, grabbing a fresh one and filling it full. "I only serve the righteous, here, no longer pirates and riffraff."

They had become friends over these many years, and that almost made up for the guilt he had over her death. It was a shame this was to be their final visit, and he aimed to make the most of it. "Have you any of that stew?" he asked, stretching conversation as long as he could.

"Of course I do!" She stepped into the kitchen while Curtis looked around.

Every grain of wood in the place and every mug behind the bar held sentimentality, and he savored every bit while he waited. She returned and placed the bowl before him, returning to her duties. He smiled down at the meal, unbothered by its lukewarm state. He never thought he would ever have come to appreciate its mere existence on the bar. He took one seemingly savory bite from the spoon, then stood.

"We must go, Ann. It's time."

"Already?" she asked. "I thought we had longer."

"No, the others are gathering, and I must take you into their realm."

"I see." She glanced nervously around the room, taking it in just as he had, with a note of finality. "Will I be afraid?" she asked.

"Only of looking upon *me*," he admitted, "but nothing will harm you so there is nothing to fear."

They stepped outside and the Ferryman resumed his form, leading her down toward the waterfront. He had been wrong, and she looked up at him with sad eyes that were not afraid at all.

"This is what their greed did to you?" she asked and he nodded his response. "Evil, the lot of them. I hope they're meant for damnation."

Judge not, he warned his friend, *or risk damnation yourself.*

She understood his meaning and made the rest of her thoughts in her mind, unaware he could read those as well.

They approached a small pier with a ferryboat tied off. On the bow, a familiar torch rested, burning with flame from another time. He waited for his fare to get settled, then pushed off from the pier. Though the water lacked current, the oars moved it along with little effort. After a while he set them to drift toward a sandy beach outside of town.

The dead had already gathered, gnashing their teeth and calling out for passage. At this, Ann became very afraid.

They will not harm you in my care, he assured her, and the woman settled.

The dead parted as the ferryboat beached, their fear of the Ferryman overcoming desperation.

He pointed at two souls huddled closely, and Elizabeth and Josiah Griggs scrambled to join Ann in the vessel. He scanned the faces for one more, choosing a sour-faced old woman with angry eyes.

She stepped right up and spat in the face of Curtis Charles. "About damned time," Molly Flannigan grumbled, sitting as far away from her granddaughter as possible. "Let's be about it, then!" she barked.

But the Ferryman did not move. He stood with two golden coins scanning the beach, waiting patiently for the final souls to arrive.

They arrived together, William Mayes and Mary Griggs.

William approached his friend first, older and weathered, wearing a weary countenance. The pirate turned tavern owner had lived out his remaining days, lamenting how he had treated his only true friend. Accepting whatever destination was meant for him, he held out two coins.

Other side, the Ferryman replied without taking the offering.

"I don't understand," William puzzled.

Always pay the Ferryman on the other side.

William sat next to the old woman who seemed genuinely to prefer a pirate over her own granddaughter's company.

The last to approach was Mary. Her beautiful hair had returned, as young and vibrant as before she had pulled it out. Her eyes, also, were whole in this form, smiling up at the boy she could have loved. Unafraid, she leaned up on tiptoes and kissed his mouth.

"I'm sorry," she whispered, her mind once again as whole as her flesh. "I was foolish to listen to Mother and more so to insist upon knowing my fate. I should have entered love blindly and experienced it with you."

Forgiven, the Ferryman answered, then helped her board the vessel.

After only a few rows they had entered open water.

"Where will you stop first?" Molly Flannigan demanded. "Will you drop me off at heaven before you condemn them all to hell?"

Before she could finish speaking, the vessel came to rest before a fiery backdrop, with tormented souls screaming eternally their master's wrath. A bony finger pointed at William Mayes who stood and nodded. He had already accepted this fate long ago. He reached into his pocket for the coins, but they had already appeared in the Ferryman's hand.

Next to disembark were Josiah and Elizabeth Griggs. They left less willingly, but the Ferryman gave them no choice but to depart the vessel. Their skin began to redden, then burst aflame without burning it away. They scrambled from the boat and into the water, finding it provided no relief. Though they tried, they could not again board the ferry.

Finally, a bony finger pointed at the old woman.

"Well, I'll be damned," the puritan declared, then magically stood on the waiting shore.

Yes, the Ferryman replied as they again shoved off, *damned for judgement of others and prideful arrogance.*

Now only two women remained, their passage long ago paid.

"I thought mine was the wrong amount?" Mary said quietly, watching her parents writhe in eternal agony.

Wrong amount... the Ferryman agreed.

"Then how?"

Suddenly Curtis Charles sat before them, wrapped in the shroud but in the form he had once worn. He only had a brief moment to appear this way and chose his words carefully. A collection of shimmering threads unfurled before him, and he ran his fingers around each as he measured their individual worth.

"The sins of the others were deliberate—betrayal, greed, judgement, and hatred. They knew their penalty and never sought forgiveness." Three of the threads abruptly burst into flames, leaving only two behind. "Your simple act of contrition and kindness on the beach did not save you from eternal damnation, it was your true repentance during your earthly torment. There is hope for your soul, Mary Griggs, and it has worth."

Tears filled her eyes and she nodded her thanks.

"What of me?" Ann Mason demanded, shocked by her destination. "I was a liar, a whore, and as guilty as Thomas Tew. I participated willingly, ruining both you and the Griggs."

"The Griggs were already ruined by their dark practices and arrogance. Their ritual locked me in this place between realms, but your sacrifice made me what I am. Tew needed a Ferryman, or the curse upon his coins would not work. But none of that was your fault. You were a victim, like me, and I forgave you the moment our spirits bonded."

Up ahead a beautiful garden emerged from the mist. Filled with the sound of birds and joyful laughter, paradise awaited the two girls. When they turned their heads to gaze upon their friend one last time, they found themselves standing on shore. Their debt to the Ferryman paid in full.

FINIS

Here is a *SNEAK PEAK*

at

Don't Pay the Ferryman

CHAPTER ONE

Castle Hills Inn, Newport, RI, 1988

Every student, teacher, parent, and alumni of Castle Hills High screamed with celebration. The homecoming game ended with a buzzer-beating seventy-yard pass from Mitch Reed to Gavin Henderson, soundly beating their rivals of Middleton. The score on the board read forty-two to zero, riling the students with the iconic *420* they had all hoped for. The principals, on the other hand, groaned at the score, fearing the number would fuel illicit recreational activities at the dance following the game. They were right, of course, and had no way to stop it.

The locker room celebrated the heroic duo as they finished with reporters and trotted up the tunnel.

"Scouts saw that performance, boys!" Coach Sanchez informed them. "Penn State, Clemson, and Wake Forest were all in the press box!" This won broad smiles from the boys, each deeply respecting their coach and appreciative of his efforts to bring the scouts to watch. David Sanchez was, in his day, best known for his work with the Dallas Cowboys. He was respected far and wide by his contacts in the sport.

Coach Sanchez pointed to the locker room. "Go get dressed, Henderson, I need to talk to Mitch."

The wide receiver nodded, grinning broadly. He was tall, well-muscled, and athletic, but had never been coach's favorite. A late arrival on the team, he barely earned playing time unless they were up by as much as they were on this night. "Thanks for putting me in tonight, Coach!" he said as he trotted off.

Sanchez waited for the boy to leave before addressing his quarterback. "What the hell *was* that out there, Mitch!"

The boy shrugged, playing dumb, but he knew. Coach had called the play as thirty-shuffle, meaning he was to throw to Sam Silver in the slot, essentially running out the clock. Instead, wanting to run up the score to impress the scouts, Mitch had thrown the fifty-seam. That put the ball in the hands of coach's least favorite receiver.

"What do you have against Henderson, Coach?" the quarterback demanded.

"Nothing! But the whole point of bringing those scouts tonight was to get you and Silver looks... not *him*! He's good, but I've invested too much in Silver to have him overlooked. That nonsense you pulled is exactly what we *don't* need! Besides, running up the score looks bad on both you *and* me as leaders. I can't have that crap on my field, Reed!"

"Sorry, Coach! I didn't mean to make you look bad. I really only wanted to make *him* look good!"

"I know he's your friend, Mitch, but keep to the game plan and only run the plays *I* call. That's how you make into the best schools and the *big* leagues!"

"I swear!" Mitch promised, then hurried to follow Gavin. They had a beach party to attend after the dance, and Molly Brown had promised to attend.

He rounded the corner and paused, shocked by what he saw. Some of his teammates had already showered and dressed for the dance and had been waiting outside the locker room. They had encircled a younger kid, someone Mitch recognized but didn't really know. He thought maybe they shared a class. He stepped up just in time to see Sam Silver give the boy a shove.

"How about it, dipshit? Why don't you watch where you're going?" the taller wide receiver demanded.

"I'm suh... sorry," the younger boy stammered. He held a black case in his hand, marking him as a member of the marching band. Mitch wasn't entirely sure but thought it may be a trombone case.

Sam homed in on it too, just as Mitch was deciding to interfere. He took it from the boy, tossing it to one of the others in the circle. Soon, it had become a game, with the football players tossing it around and the band boy jumping to grab it. He never had a chance against the bigger, more athletic boys.

Mitch was just about to say something to end their fun when another voice called out, "Hey! Stop being jackasses!" Gavin shouted to his teammates.

Sam Silver whirled around to face off, not bothering to catch the trombone flying toward him. It sailed past, crashing to the ground and popping open on the ground. The smaller boy rushed to check on his instrument while Mitch stepped up beside Gavin.

"What the hell, Sam?" Mitch demanded. "Since when are you a bully?"

"Since you started throwing bombs to your new best friend!" Silver growled with a spat toward Gavin.

Mitch started to step forward, but Gavin held out a hand to stop him. "If you've got a problem with me, Silver, let's iron it out now!"

Sam stepped forward, ready to fight, but Gavin stepped between them. "Same team, guys! What the hell? Do you want coach to bench us all for fighting *and* bullying?" To Sam he added, "I gave him a bomb so he can get some stats, not take your starting job or scout glory! Besides, you've already committed to UMASS. We're a *team*, and everyone deserves a shot!"

This settled Sam, taking away a bit of his anger.

Gavin, too, had cooled, and knelt down to help the band kid with his case. "What's your name, kid?" he asked.

"Peter Mayes," the boy replied shyly.

Mitch watched as Sam and the others walked away, the wide receiver flipping them off as he did, and waited till they were out of earshot. "Peter Mayes like the guy who owns Castle Hills Inn?" Mitch asked, a bit surprised. If so, this kid was from one of the richest families in Rhode Island. They owned the place where the homecoming dance was about to be held.

"Yeah," Peter replied, that's my dad.

"Sorry they roughed you up, Peter," Mitch said honestly. "Hey, I know! Some of us guys are skipping out during the dance tonight. We're gonna light a bonfire on the beach and have our own party. Why don't you come?"

Peter's eyes followed Sam and the others disappearing down the tunnel. "I dunno," he said, "I don't really belong with you guys."

"Sam won't be there," Gavin assured him. "Trust me, if he's gonna be there, you can bet *I* won't!"

"Seriously," Mitch added, "the rest of our friends are cool. You can even bring a girl if you want."

Peter blushed. "I don't really know any."

Mitch and Gavin exchanged a look, trying hard not to laugh but both ready to boost the kid's confidence at the party.

"Don't worry about that, then," Mitch said slyly, "we'll introduce you to plenty at the party!"

"We'll see," the boy said, then hurried down the corridor, going the opposite way from Sam.

"He ain't comin' at all," Mitch said with a chuckle.

"A six-pack says he does," Gavin said with a smile. "Who *wouldn't* want to hang out with us and all the cheerleaders?"

Mitch smiled, thinking about Molly Brown and the tight sweater she'd be wearing to the party. "No doubt. We *know* how to have a good time."

Continued in Don't Pay the Ferryman!

FERRYMAN

A LETTER FROM T.B. PHILLIPS

What a change from my normal routine!

When Chris Hays and McLain McGuire of Charter Comics first approached me outside of Cowtown ComiCon, I was immediately intrigued by whatever project they offered. Fellow Creators, the visionaries behind several successful Indie Comics, true entrepreneurs, and all around great guys, I agreed right away!

I knew, of course, about the Ferryman series and loved the story, the artwork, and the passion behind the project. Just the opportunity to work with Chris and Charter Comics' creators drew me in for serious consideration of whatever was offered. When Chris asked me to deliver a novelized version of *Don't Pay the Ferryman*, I did not even hesitate to give him a resounding, "Yes!"

Raised reading the greats like King and Koontz, I always wanted to try my hand in the Horror genre, and my only worry was whether or not this story would live up to Charter Comics expectations. But Chris trusted me completely with his story and gave me free reign to further develop Curtis Charles, Mary Griggs, and all the other wonderful characters he created.

I hope you enjoyed my rendition of *Don't Pay the Ferryman*, a careful blend of Horror, Historical Fiction, and Pirates! I thoroughly enjoyed this project and have many more ideas to add to this amazing creation. I promised Chris one novel, but there *will* be another Ferryman story in the near future! Who knows... I may have begun writing it already!

If you enjoyed this story, it would help if you left a kind and honest review wherever it is found.

Books by T.B. Phillips are found
everywhere books are sold or by visiting
AndalonStudios.com

Andalon Saga

Andalon Origins
Andalon Project (April 2022)
Andalon Paradox (Expected Spring 2023)
Dreamers of Andalon
Andalon Awakens (June 2019)
Andalon Arises (July 2020)
Andalon Attacks (December 2020)
Children of Andalon
Andalon Legacy (September 2022)

Chilling Tales

Ferryman (October 2022)

Corrupted Realms

Wailing Tempest (April 2021)
Howling Shadow (September 2021)